CHILDREN OF THE WIND

CHILDREN OF THE WIND

The combined journals
of Cully and Doc

Ed Sundt

To order additional copies of this book, contact:
Xlibris Corporation
1-888-795-4274
www.Xlibris.com
Orders@Xlibris.com
124876

CONTENTS

PART I
Eleven Begins

PART II
"Memory believes before knowing remembers."

PART III
Passages

PART IV
The Letter

PART V
The Journey

PART VI
Home Again

PART VII
Mergings

"There is a Catskill eagle in some souls that can alike dive down into the blackest gorges, and soar out of them again and become invisible in the sunny spaces. And even if he forever flies within the gorge, that gorge is in the mountains; so that even in his lowest swoop the mountain eagle is still higher than other birds upon the plain, even though they soar."

Herman Melville, <u>Moby Dick</u>

ACKNOWLEDGMENTS

I wish to acknowledge the following as contributing ideas which were most useful in creating certain scenes in this story:

for family background: the Strongsville, Ohio, branch of the Cuyahoga County Library where I found the volumes entitled <u>The History of the Descendants of Elder John Strong of Northampton, Mass.</u> (Benjamin W. Dwight 1871, reprinted 1975) which provided me with background on the family with which I have become very familiar;

for information on the National Road: details and anecdotes about the National Road can be found at greater length in Norris F. Schneider's booklet entitled <u>The National Road, Main Street of America</u>, published by the Ohio Historical Society, 1987 (second edition);

for information on the Hartford circus fire: R. T. Brown and the Newspaper Collectors Society of America, used with their permission. They may be reached via the Internet at http://www.historybuff.com/library/index.html ;

for the Thoreau passage: Henry David Thoreau's <u>Walden</u> ;

for background on the orphan trains: accounts of the orphan trains can be found in several sources, including an illustrated article "It took trains to put street kids on the right track out of the slums" by Donald Dale Jackson, published in the August, 1986, *Smithsonian*, volume 17, Number 5.

Discovering the Children of the Wind

Two days after Grandma Anna Strong's funeral, I was designated to be the family member who would go through her things and make an inventory for the estate. The old furniture, which I had dreaded doing, took only two days. The contents of her desk, which I expected to be a brief listing, took several weeks.

And that's my story.

The journals which I found there became the focus of my life, and they form the body of this tale. There were also a few letters, a certificate of death for her son, my father John; forty or fifty snapshots, some money—thirteen one dollar bills—hidden in a secret vertical drawer of the desk, a set of keys for locks now unknown, a hand-written poem to her father, and a single yellowed piece of paper on which was written in smudged pencil the name Augustus Jared Strong.

These journals speak for themselves, literally, as the two writers take turns telling their story. The pages so captivated my imagination that I searched to fill in their gaps and even fancied that I could solve some of the riddles that they posed, questions left unanswered, moments left unrecorded. I have added chapters which, although technically fictional, are based on interviews and further reading of diaries, aged newspaper columns, and even town records which complete further the histories of the people we see here.

My task became both research and creation, and this volume is the result, a story which begins in the hot farmland of south-central Illinois in the mid-1930's.

Augustus Strong, II

PART I

Eleven Begins

CHAPTER 1

Cully

I sit the jug down on the dry, bleached well-boards, push up the hot, iron pump handle with both hands, and jump into the air to let my weight help pull the handle down. My shirt flaps against my sweaty back.

Deep in the well a pipe gurgles, and I jump again to draw the gray handle down. The first clear trickle from the spout misses the jug's small mouth, and I push it over with my foot. Now water gushes with each downstroke, most of it splashing into the old glass bottle Pa calls a jug.

High up, a hawk circles over us, not even flapping his wings but just still, floating, riding the air.

I like the squeak of the handle and the soft, wet water sound. When I'm finished, I'll splash some on my head and neck.

"What's your Pa up to?" rasps Aunt Clara from the house. I look back at her, misty behind the dirty screen of the back door, then out into the heat-wavering land where Pa and the mule are working the late field, the patch he always turns last in the season. He'd said when we finished that I could have a piece of the candy Mrs. McKinnon brought for my tenth birthday.

I squint and make out two shapes against the dry, yellow-red field and bright white sky. The mule has his head dropped, unmoving but in harness. And Pa, kneeling, weight forward on his hands.

"What's he up to?" she asks again, but not to me.

"He must be looking at somethin'," I say toward Aunt Clara's dim face.

"Something's wrong !" she yells.

I look back to where I am to tote the water to Pa. Neither shape has moved. A fear hurts my chest. "Pa?" I'm running now and I see the kneeling figure slowly tip over on his side and lie still in the hot dirt.

"Pa !" I call again, stumbling over uneven rows. My hat falls off. Small clods of dirt get into my shoes and crumble, hurting. The mule lifts a rear hoof and shivers the flies off his haunch. I hear Aunt Clara coming behind me, calling, yelling, screaming.

We get to Pa and turn him on his back, and I stand in the sun's way to make a shadow on his face. Aunt Clara touches his lips, kneels down and listens at his mouth, slaps his stubbly cheek.

"How c'd ya leave him alone on such a day?" She gives me such a look. "Whyn't ya stay with him?"

I don't know what she means. She scares me. "He sent me to fill the jug." My tears stain his grimy undershirt in blacker drops than sweat or dirt. I shout across at her look, but my voice isn't strong and each word separates, sobs out in gulps of breath, *"He . . . sent . . . me !"*

"You!" she says. I don't know if she means me or Pa. "This! Now this! Now they're both gone!" She lowers her face against him and screams into his chest, "No!"

She stands, shaking her head as if she is angry. Her face is crooked in my tears. His arm feels strange, warm but soft and weak. Oh, Pa. I sink down against him, putting my hands on his shoulders, my head under his chin, and squeeze my eyes shut. The sun beats on my back.

When I lift my head again and wipe my eyes, Aunt Clara is not there. What would he want me to do? I try to move him, but he is too heavy. So I just stand up and look around. Then I unhitch the mule and lead it back to the yard, wanting it to hurry so's I can get back to tend him. "Always put things away," he had said.

The jug of water is still at the well, shining in the sun. The raised gray pump handle points toward the field, toward Pa. I drop the reins and run to the jug. Again and again in my head I say, "He sent me." I snatch up the jug by the little round handle at the neck and run back toward Pa. I stoop to pick up my hat and then I reach him.

I kneel beside Pa again and wet my hands with the cooling water, rubbing the dirt off his face. My shirt-tail wipes the water from his cheeks and chin and throat. It is hard to get it all where he has whiskers. Then I take my hat and set it over his face. It's almost too small, the hat Aunt Clara made fun of me for when I picked it out in town: "Two-gallon lid for a half-pint," she said. Pa had told her to be still.

Back near the still house the dark mule stands, stomping.

I know I can't stay there now. I walk slowly, a little dust swirling up ahead in the heat, and go out across the fields away from the house to try to find a road. The dirt still hurts in my shoes.

CHAPTER 2

Doc

I had driven past him earlier that morning as I went south. Now, returning, he was only about a mile further along the road. He was about eleven or twelve, and his slow walk—more of a trudge, really—was, in fact, without direction. His head was down; his feet scuffed along. The hot, flat farmland made him seem a speck.

I pulled to the side perhaps fifty yards ahead of him, wiped the sweat from my face, and watched him in the dusty side mirror. He looked almost like a mirage as he moved toward me through the heat rising from the hot, dry road between us. His blue shirt hung unbuttoned, and his small steps raised puffs of dust as he approached without seeming to notice that I had stopped.

A high yellow-white sun baked the windless land, yet he trudged along hatless, hands stuffed into the worn pockets of his trousers. His hay-colored hair lay flat, uncombed, unimportant. No sign indicated that he even saw the car, yet he moved out to go around it on my side, not looking up the empty road.

"Need a lift?" I asked as he scuffed past my window, nearly brushing my arm. No answer. Although there was no one between us and the yellow horizon, he did not seem to realize that I was speaking to him. "You need a lift, son?"

He stopped and turned to look at me, considering me, his head tilted to one side, his dark eyes squinting from under lowered eyebrows. His dirty cheeks had two clear trails down them; his open shirt had no buttons; his shoes were scraped light and raw on the toes. He still did not answer but slowly swung his foot in an arc in the yellow-brown dust.

"I'm going to Weed if you need a lift. Where you headed?"

His thin shoulders shrugged quickly, hands still jammed deep into his pockets. His too-large belt lapped out in front of his hip like a thirsty dog's tongue.

"Come on," I said. "Wherever you're going, it's too hot to walk there." We were fifteen miles from the next town; five at least from any farmhouse. I pulled my bag closer to me so there would be room on the seat.

He moved slowly around the front of the car to the other side, dragging a finger through the dust without interest, marking a blue line on the fender. He pulled down hard on the door handle, and I reached across and opened it for him. He got in and, using both hands, pulled the door shut.

As we drove, he sat far from me on the front seat, against the door, his thin arms resting in his lap, his dusty palms cupped. He looked out the side window, his chin barely above the sill.

"Any place special?" I asked, and knew before he shook his head that our first stop would be the diner in Weed. "How far've you come? From Wilson?"

"Marston," he answered with soft sharpness, naming a town thirty miles to the south. I knew that wasn't true. He sat motionless, his skin dimmed by hours of dirt roads.

As we drove, dust bloomed behind us, drifting whitely across into the corn and wheat fields. I heard no sound from him and I did not speak for some time. Then I turned to glance at him: his head was in his hands and his body shook with silent sobs.

CHAPTER 3

Doc

The drive was quiet then. He had sat staring out the side window, saying nothing. I drove toward Weed not knowing what to do after that. I felt anxious in a way I did not understand, hurrying against that immense weight I always felt when an animal was sick and no one knew what to do and I had to drive many miles to try to stave off its dying for another month or year. Usually the word came late, some younger member of the farm family riding out to my house to "Fetch the Doc" after waiting had failed and home tonics had failed. Then into the car and hurrying, that hollow weight bearing down in my chest. The feeling of helplessness; the need to try.

Far ahead was the tall black bulk of a grain elevator, the first imperfection on the smoothness of the bright horizon. Weed. Even as we drew nearer to the town and five or six small, simple houses appeared, he did not seem to look at any specific thing. His head was stationary and things passed him, sweeping across his field of vision and out, gone, not even recorded.

The diner was part way down the single street. Weed was an old-looking, plain, gray town, a packed dirt street up a slight rise and down into the prairie again. The road immediately left behind the little cluster of practical wooden buildings: hardware, post office, livery, feed and grain, an all-purpose store with everything from remedies to yard goods to work shoes, a small diner which also served, in the back, as a saloon, its two parts distinct and separated by an archway with a green curtain hung from dark, wooden rings on a metal rod.

Weed was on the way to other places; it was seldom anyone's destination. Yet its location seemed to be at least right for enough business or close enough for an excuse to "go into town," a trip that was, in fact, an escape from the repetition of chores and seasons, crops and weather, and the hard, sharp winters which sometimes made you think life stopped, just as if people and animals could hibernate and reappear in the spring.

They couldn't, and winters especially were the breaking time. Everyone could struggle against the heat or the unrelenting hardness of farm work; there was the one common bond in that, somehow, a stubborn acknowledgment of choice. If people broke, they were probably broken by the freezing power of winter isolation, even though the breakage might not appear on the surface for many months.

The breaking took many forms, none of which anyone really understood. The local newspaper generally reported the insanity, the disappearance, the suicide, the arson; sometimes it attributed causes, such as poverty or the death of a child. I had seen a few of those lives, hardscrabble lives scratched out with scrawny cows and a lame mule, evaporating into the dry prairie wind and forgotten, the empty frame house drying, shrinking, too, into the vast, level, and glaring land, the only reminders for a few years being a splintered, stationary windmill or a loosely boarded hole in the earth where someone had attempted a well. The fences, forlorn and broken, separated nothing any longer.

Sometimes the people just left, vanished, walked off to die alone or packed up to return to what had not been good enough before, the promise broken. Some left, of course, in coffins, especially the children, victims of influenza, pox, scarlet fever, beatings, undernourishment, frail victims of someone's frustrations or undiscriminating and wind-blown sickness. Their open coffins were propped up against the wall and they were given a final—and perhaps first—photograph, with finest white clothing and the small hands together, their delicate and vulnerable beauty so fragile and sad.

I sensed that some death, some abandonment had happened here: I felt the inner pressure, the helplessness, the need to try. The boy remained silent.

I pulled in in front of the diner. "Lunch" said the sign, black paint on white boards. Our dust drifted past us. Someone near the hardware store stopped, turned to look, and then went on. A thin, long-legged dog moved past after sniffing at the tires and wetting one.

"Come on, let's get some food," I said. His hand moved toward the door handle, stopped, and returned to his lap. "It's OK," I said.

"We'll just get some food. Ever been here?"

He nodded slightly, his eyes looking to the right toward the store, and again he put his hand on the handle, pressed down hard, and opened the door.

Each store had its own brief board porch, with the spaces between stores again simply dirt. Out in front of the store on a plank bench sat the usual two men, Evan Bender and Eliphalet Armitage. They nodded 'hello' as we passed, watching as if concerned with details. The boy trailed me to the diner, waited for me to go in, then followed.

We moved from the bright mid-day sun into the dimness of the room, my eyes adjusting to the shift. Two brown ceiling fans rotated slowly and hanging rolls of yellow fly paper swayed between them, a few flies struggling against the gummy strip. The room was narrow, with a short white counter on the right and four or five dark wooden booths to the left, a narrow aisle between the counter stools and the booths. The pattern continued on the other side of the green curtain, and, in slow times, the bartender in the saloon was also the cook and waiter in the diner, his area not being divided by the curtain.

"How about here?" I said, indicating a booth. He slid into the other side. The scarred yellowed menu, tucked behind the sugar and salt and pepper, was worn and simple, and I handed the boy one. "Get anything you want." He opened it but did not read it. "Want a sandwich?"

He nodded that he did, and I ordered sandwiches and milk for both of us. He looked even younger now as he sat there, yet his hands had small calluses and other signs of work. "Well, what shall I call you? Where're you headed?"

His answer was a brief lifting of his shoulders: don't know. I took that as an answer to the second question and as a good sign. "My name's Gunnar," I said, "but people call me 'Doc.' I doctor sick animals, mostly around Plaut Junction and Weed. Had a call to make down toward Wilson, so I passed you this morning going down. You were still walking when I came back, so I thought you might like a ride." This time I stuck my arm across the table, hand out. "What's yours?"

The dark fan blades slowly whirred. I heard someone go out and the screen door, pulled by its little spring, banged shut. He weakly shook my hand and almost spoke, but he looked beyond me and the booth, down the aisle toward the front door. His eyes showed fear, his hand slipped out of mine, and he slid out of his seat and ran toward the back of the diner, through the green curtain and into the saloon.

"Hey !" shouted the man behind the counter, and he began to move after the boy.

"I'll get him," I said, and brushed the curtain up with an arm as I went through.

CHAPTER 4

Cully

I begin to feel lost.

A man gives me a ride to Weed and we go into the diner for some food. I can't talk to him even when he asks me questions, and I don't want to tell him, but I can't tell him about Pa or Aunt Clara or the mule or the hat or anything.

He's acting nice, and it isn't until I sit in the booth that I feel how thirsty I am. I drink one glass of water but I spill some on my hand and it looks just like the well water and makes it hard for me to breathe.

I thought leaving was best, and now I feel like I can't go back. She'll tan me good like she did the day the clothes pole snapped under the heavy load and the wash dragged in the dirt on the sagging line. She said I'd set the pole wrong. Every day there'll be just her there. And I know how she'll be after me. I can hear her scolding. There's too much I don't do right.

He says, "Well, what's your name?" and tells me his. Says to call him Doc. I never seen Doc before, but he's nice. Pa spoke about a man named "Doc" once, but I never seen him.

The room has a shelf of glasses on one side, just under some round white globes, and when I look across at them I can see the spinning fans and the white-squared ceiling in the mirror. The big fans click and sway, and they have greasy-looking yellow fly strips hanging down.

He asks again what is my name and he reaches across the table to shake hands. I know he won't grab me 'cause he's had chances to do that. I shake his hand. A silver coin spins and settles in quick, rolling circles on the counter as a man pays change for his meal. The man goes out and the screen door slams.

I start to tell Doc my name, but when I look past his arm I see a woman standing there. She's just outside, but she has her hands cupped by her face and is trying to squint through the screen door into the diner without having to come in. Her face doesn't show, just a black shape beyond and pressing on the screen, but she's peering in, searching for somebody. I slide fast off the seat and run past the green curtain into the back room and hide down behind the end of the counter. I know it is Aunt Clara.

He finds me right away and somehow he seems to know that I don't want her to see me. He talks to me for a while and doesn't try to take me back to the front of the diner, just talks in the dim, empty back room.

The waiter looks past the curtain and then comes back there with us. "Is he okay, Doc?" he asks. Doc sort of signals him with a nod and tells him he can go back out front.

I feel like that small brown rabbit that we trapped once in the shed. It darted and darted and then just stopped in a corner. It put its ears down against its back, its nose kept moving, and its eyes looked away from us at the wall. We could see its heart or breath moving its chest in and out real fast. Pa spoke to it, and he told me how scared it was, and even though it had been stealing some of our plants, he just left it there and we went back outside. I've never seen an animal so scared. When I went back later, it was still there.

Doc sits down beside me on the floor and he seems able to tell how I feel. He seems cool and strong.

"Well," he says, "you're a mighty fast mover for a tired boy. So ? . . . what is your name? You can tell me now. Whoever you thought you saw is gone."

I look at the curtain, trying to hear beyond it. There's no woman's voice. "John Culbertson," I say to him.

"Do people call you John?" he asks.

"No . . . Cully," I tell him.

"Good. Cully." He waits. We sit there quiet with the noises from the diner coming into the darkened part. "How you doing? Okay?"

I nod.

"Better tell me what's going on now so we can decide what to do next."

I stay quiet.

"It's okay. Look, I'm not going to take you back to wherever you walked away from until you say so, so let me know what's happening. I can help you better."

It is hard to tell him about this morning, and my words don't sound strong. I just tell that Pa died in the field. He listens and nods and then rubs the back of my head and neck and doesn't say anything. I keep thinking that I will cry, but it never comes and I feel just dry inside my cheeks, as if there's no tears left inside. But my chest hurts as if the whole thing is happening all over again.

When I stop, we sit still for a long time it seems. I can hear people talking out in the diner, sometimes laughing, and dishes clattering on each other or thumping when they're set down on the tables, and the fans' hum.

All he says is a long, soft, sad word: "Well" and he breathes out. Then he asks, "So you thought you saw someone?"

I nod.

"From home? Coming after you?"

I nod.

"You know, they couldn't have gotten here that fast." Then he waits a while. "Why don't you come spend some time with me for a few days, and we'll talk about what to do next?"

I see for the first time that I don't know what I am going to do. I just wanted to get away, get to a town. He's younger than Pa, and not so big, but he seems like him in some ways.

I nod, and we push up off the floor and go back through the curtain and into the diner. We even sit again in the same booth. The waiter comes back over and says, "I kept your food ready in the ice box, Doc. Here it is." And he looks at me and smiles at Doc and sets the sandwiches down in front of each of us, with a knife and fork and spoon and napkin and a glass of cold milk.

"Another stray?" the waiter asks.

"Yeah, sort of," says Doc. Then, "After we eat, we'll go next door to the store and get you a hat."

CHAPTER 5

Doc

While the boy was sorting through the hats in Walker's store, I went back to talk to Lem Briskman in the post office, just a walled off corner of the store, with a window and many small boxes which had numbered glass in the front so a person could see whether he had mail or not.

Lem was heavy, black haired, bespectacled, someone who had started as a helper in the post office and had done the rural route himself until the postmaster died; then Lem took over and a younger man did the route. All most people saw of him now was his head peering through the grillwork and his hand and arm passing mail out to them.

The farms were so widespread that the mail was sent out west and south on one day, north and east on the next, so one week your farm could get mail twice a week and the next week three times. It didn't go out on Saturday except for something special.

To say "you would get mail" really means that the mailman would go past your place. Not many people actually got mail often except those who lived right in Weed and walked to the post office. And if the mail truck was late, the store would have several people standing around, mainly for gossip but partly in the half-hope that a letter or a Sears and Roebuck or a Montgomery Wards catalog might come.

The mail route seemed to head off into the remote distance, as if the carrier were heading toward the end of the earth. His dusty car churned out into the silence and he was gone, vanishing behind the rise while his dust faded to the color of the sky. He usually pulled back in in mid-afternoon in time to sort the next mail into the pockets in the big canvas sheet that he used, rolling it so that he could unwind it across the back seat the next day with the right pockets reachable for the next people on the route. The pockets had no names unless the farm was a large and enduring one, sure to be there next month. Nearly each vertical row of pockets had one of those, perhaps, the other nameless pockets silently acknowledging the transience and riskiness of such life.

"Lem," I said, "is Matthew heading out south tomorrow?"

He glanced over from his work desk to see who was asking. "Afternoon, Doc. Yep."

"Could he check the Culbertson place, do you think? Does he know that farm?"

"He knows it. If not, he'll find it."

"The boy is here. I think he ran away. Have Matthew tell them he is here with me. Tell them the boy is all right."

"Sure thing," he said. "Just jot it here on this piece of paper and I'll see that Matthew takes it."

I wrote it out, not saying much more than that the boy was safe and should I bring him home. I knew that the phone line had not reached there yet, and this was the quickest way to get them word and stop their worry.

My request was not unusual in an area of Rural Free Delivery. The letter carrier not only took parcels and letters and circulars, he also spread general news, he delivered crates of chicks, shipments of seed, and he frequently was a lifeline for people without telephones and too remote to send out word that some sort of assistance was needed. Some years back, lots of people wouldn't have known that the Unites States had been at war if they hadn't had a chance to chat with the mailman every other day. Often, after I had tended a sick cow or horse, I would check up with the healing by way of Matthew rather than drive all the way out just to find out that the animal had recovered or died.

There was no hurry. One learned that out here. It was a steady pace but slow, bound to the weather and the seasons, with no more hurry about human birth or death than the slow growth of a seed into a cornstalk. It was not uncommon for a farm woman to give birth almost as one of the day's chores, feeding the calves, doing the wash, making bread, giving birth, making dinner.

Death, too, became part of the accepted schedule, infrequent but not unexpected even when sudden and tragic; just another fact. Only newcomers had a hard time with that, and it was even sadly true that in many large families, the death of the mule was more crucial and more of a concern than the death of one of the children.

But the death or desertion of a father with young children and a farm to tend was a potential disaster. A woman could become a withered figure of stringy muscle and baked skin on such a farm, surviving on sheer pluck but old at thirty and dead herself at forty. One life-saving solution was to board, send, sell, give the children to other families and to leave, often for some imagined place of betterment in the West. I knew that a surprisingly large number of the people moving out West were single women, women alone and willing to set a seal over the past for the chance to have a hope in the future.

I didn't know what had happened to Cully's mother, but Aunt Clara was now in that position: a few acres that seemed like a big farm, probably had little knowledge of how to work it, and someone else's boy to care for. When I picked up my unopened letter five days later, I knew what Matthew's answer would be before he gave it: a fresh grave out back, the mule and wagon gone, the house empty.

Clara had sealed the past and left.

CHAPTER 6

Cully

He takes me to his house, a small, flat farmhouse in a T shape, with a barn and some sheds out back and off to the side. He has a cow, two calves, two horses, a goat, some chickens, and a dog. The calves and the two horses have been sick, and he tends them here and then sends them back to their owners, though most of the animals he tends just stay on their farms.

Besides the chickens and the goat and dog, the yard has some trees in it, which seems different for me, and a long, dirt driveway which leads up to a side entrance that goes into the kitchen. Off that and leading out the back is what he calls his office, where he has shelves and cabinets for his medical supplies, and a roll-top desk.

He tells me what's happened, that Aunt Clara's gone, and he says we should go down there and get what I need because I will stay with him for a while.

The ride back takes longer than I expect. It's hard to believe that it is so far. I never noticed it when I was walking. The houses are far apart and the dry road just seems to go on and on.

We don't talk during the ride. He stops at the market and gets some boxes which are in the back seat in case we want to move some things. He says we'll leave it mostly alone because Aunt Clara might come back and need the things. He says we'll leave a note explaining where I am and that I am staying with him. I don't think she will come back.

He'd showed me a little piece he was to put into the weekly newspaper saying where I was and how to find me if anybody needed to. "That all right with you?" he'd asked. "At least they'll know I didn't kidnap you," he grinned.

"I did that when Beans and Macawber came here, so I guess I should do it for you, too."

"Beans" is his dog, a middle-sized, short-haired white dog with lots of small brown and black spots that look like beans. "Macawber" is his goat, a skinny, white and gray, nosy animal with a small beard. He comes into my room sometimes and sniffs around my clothes and I have to shoo him back outside before he starts eating anything. Both Beans and Macawber were strays.

He found Beans by the side of the road about three years ago, Doc says, her feet torn from walking and just about dead from no water or food. Doc said he lifted her into the back seat and brought her home. Beans sleeps by my bed and during the night grinds away at a big bone she likes.

Macawber was standing "out in the middle of nowhere," and he didn't run when Doc went to him and took hold of the rope that was hanging from around his neck. Brought him back, too, and never found anyone that said they'd lost him. "Probably was on the back of someone's wagon or truck that was passing through and just saw something nice and said, 'Excuse me' and jumped off," that's what Doc said.

He smiles a lot and his house is comfortable. I am learning how to help him with his chores, too, which are mostly different from the ones on our farm. He doesn't grow much, just a small patch for his vegetables, but he tends the animals a lot. He even has to drive to people's farms to help them with their animals or to slaughter a pig or birth a calf. He's going to show me how he works in his blacksmith shop, too.

When our farm comes into sight, I don't recognize it at first. He spots the name on the old, dented mailbox. "Over there," he says, motioning out his window at a building in the distance. It is very small and dark against the land, and I get up on my knees on the seat to see better. Then I can tell it's the same house and shed that I used to look back at when we were in the fields, its stumpy black chimney at one end. The closer we get, the stiller it seems, no motion, no sounds. There's a pole along the drive that was to be for electricity, but it never got hooked up. Just a pole standing there.

We stop beside the gray house and he calls "Hello?" but there's no answer. I look for someone to come to the window, but nobody does. We get out and walk around to the front and go in. The door's not latched. I'm not used to going in that way because most of the time we just went in and out the kitchen. He'd said the house was empty, but it's not. Everything is there, even the piano that Ma had brought when they moved out here. Doc lifts the cover back. Lots of the keys are chipped, and some look brownish. When he touches a few of the keys, the sound wavers and is old, not good notes.

"Can you play this?" he asks, turning his head to me without taking his hand off the keys.

"No. Ma used to. It's just sat with that shawl on it since then."

"Hamilton Piano Co., Limited, London," he says, looking at the fancy gold swirls of writing on the front, just below the drawing of two gold lions snarling at each other over a red shield.

We walk through, past an open door leading to a bedroom, and I can see sunlight in there and a bed with the light blue covers loose and rumpled on it, hanging down partly on the floor. In the kitchen, the wood stove is cold, the kindling box only half full. In the middle of the wood-plank floor is the table with red and white checked oilcloth on it, worn and darkened in places, one edge uneven where we cut off a piece once to patch the screen door. A spoon is on the table. A green, chipped plate is tilted on edge in the first sink.

Beside the door hangs the strap she used.

He stands at the back door for a minute, looking through the screen. Then he goes outside and I hear a few steps off to the side yard. "Cully," he says. He has come back to the screen door and is looking in, talking through the screen. He says softly, "Your Pa's grave is here. You should come see it."

I look through the door. Way out in the field, the plow still tilts on its side, one handle flat on the ground and the other poking up at an angle into the air, and near it the water jug gleams in the sunlight. My hat isn't there. The wind might've carried it away. Closer in I see the grave, back past the well toward the shed.

It's a mound of dirt, almost like part of the field he was working, just humped up in one spot. We walk out to it. There's a short stick jabbed into one end and tacked on it is a piece of cardboard that says his name, John M. Culbertson, Jr., and his years, written in pencil. Nothing else. It doesn't say who dug it. The writing gets blurry.

"I'll go look in the shed," he says. "You can stay here." And I hear his steps go off as I look at the long, thin mound.

I don't really want to stay there. First I look around, not really looking for anything but just seeing it. I kneel down by the grave as I know I should do, but I don't know what to pray and I feel ashamed because my thoughts remember lots of things and I don't think just about him. The only sound is the hot wind, and I can feel my hair move. After a few minutes, I hear some hammering from the shed and I look there, but Doc's still inside and the noise comes through the open door.

I put my hand on the mound and it is warm and dry. I pick up a small clump of the soil and crumble it slowly between both hands onto the grave, the dust blowing away before it lands, then I rub my hands back and forth over the mound to smooth it out carefully. A crow caws as it flies over.

It's hard not to cry, even though Pa always said not to, that I must be big. My tears drop onto the dirt of the mound and make dark stains in the earth that sink in and then lighten and are gone. They blend right into the grave. And I get a feeling that it's better now. Somehow the tears fading into the earth of Pa's grave make me feel calmer.

When Doc comes back, I stand up and brush my hands off on my pants. He has a flat board with a stake nailed to the back, and he has used some of the brown paint from the work shed to paint my pa's name and years on it, but he has added "R.I.P." and he tells me that means "Rest In Peace."

"Here," he says, handing me the hammer. Its claw end is heavy, but the wooden handle is worn smooth and dark. "Why don't you tap this into the ground there," and he pulls out the other stick with the cardboard. "Be careful not to touch the paint," he says. I sit the end of the new stake in the hole and hit the top of it with the flat of the hammer, and it drives into the hole and becomes firm.

"All right," he says, and he takes the hammer from me and hits the stake two or three more times to be sure it is in solid. Then we stand up and back away a step or two and look at the grave again.

"Come on," he says, after a minute, "let's get your things," and when we turn back to the house, I stop because I think I am going to see Aunt Clara standing behind the screen door, watching, and I can feel a fear in my throat. But she's not there.

He sets the stick and cardboard on the sink bench and writes a note on the back of the cardboard telling where I am. He also leaves his letter there. Then he says "Where's your room?" and waits for me to lead him.

It's not my room, really, just sort of the side of a little room off the parlor where they keep other things, some wooden crates, a broom and dust pan, two open and half-empty red boxes of shotgun shells, some old newspapers, a chest-of-drawers with nails and bolts and hooks and rusty screwdrivers and things like that on it. There's a sprung mouse trap on the floor with a bits of dried cheese still on the tongue. The big trunk with winter clothes is against the far wall, its black lid shut down but not tight, not locked. A yellow shade hangs half way down one window at an angle because I never am able to get it to roll back up straight, its draw strings broken in two uneven lengths and the round crocheted pull-ring gone. My bed is a mattress on the floor with the bed clothes still messy and loose. I look back at Doc.

"Why don't you get a couple boxes from the car. I'll look around a bit and see if there's any perishables we should take," and he lifts up a part of the pile of newspapers, sees the ones underneath, and lets them fall again by rippling them down slowly, watching the main words or maybe the dates . . . or maybe nothing at all.

I run out the back door to the car and get two boxes. It's only when I start back that I realize I should've used the front door, so I go back in that way. He tells me to pack up what I want.

There's not much to get. Two work shirts and one good one that's getting kind of small, another pair of pants, some socks that don't match, my maroon winter coat, a long belt. I fold it all into the box and look through the black trunk and the chest-of-drawers to see if there's anything else. There's some letters, a small harmonica, and a chipped little round magnifying glass. My broken jack knife isn't there.

It's hard to do.

"Is this your mother?" says his voice behind me, and when I turn around I see that he's holding her picture facing me. It's in a silvery frame that's dull, and the picture is brownish on the edges."

"Yes," I say. She is wearing all white, with a white hat tilted back on her head so that her long black hair shows. It's only the upper half of her, but she seems to be sitting, and behind her is a fence and some trees and bushes. Pa told me once that the trees weren't really there, that the picture was taken in a room and it's really just a painting on the wall behind her. But she's smiling and looks very pretty. I've looked at the picture many times.

"Want to take this, too?" he asks.

I nod.

"Anything else? Any books or anything? Shoes?" he asks. There isn't anything else except stuff that was Pa's or some old furniture that we didn't use much 'cause we mostly sit in the kitchen on the wooden chairs. There aren't any books. So we leave everything else. He didn't find anything in the ice box that was any good, but he did heave some rotten things out the back.

We get in the car and head back to his house.

"You don't have to tell me this if you don't feel like it, but were you there when your dad died?"

"Yes."

"Can you tell me more about what happened?"

"He was working in the field and he just fell down and died."

"Was your Aunt Clara there?"

"Yes. She came out. I was getting water in the jug and she saw him and yelled. She kept yelling and we went to where Pa was, but he was gone already. I covered his face with my hat. She went somewhere, I don't know where. Back to the house, I think."

"And you left then? Walked to the road and left?"

"Yes."

"And I came along. Good thing, wasn't it? Where were you headed?"

"I don't know." I shrug. "Nowhere."

PART II

"Memory believes
before knowing remembers."

William Faulkner, <u>Light in August</u>

CHAPTER 7

Doc

Taking him back to that house was like probing into a strange and mysterious other world. I did not know what we would find, I didn't know how he would react, and all the time we were there I sensed that I was an intruder and might be challenged suddenly by a voice and a shotgun. It was an uneasy time, especially when we were out by the grave.

And then finding his mother's picture.

It was face down in the piano bench with a film of dust on it. On the back of it, written in gold on the thick, gray cardboard, it named a photographic studio in Willimantic, Connecticut, and a chill had gone through me at this dark and murky memory of a section of the country that had once been a part of my childhood, now so vague and lost that seeing it written was almost like hearing a noise far off and then not really being sure you had heard it at all, wondering where it was and what it had been. No image returned with the sensation of the name.

The woman in the picture was dark and beautiful, posed slightly turned to the side, demure, intelligent seeming, and, I would guess, somewhat embarrassed by the formality of the posing and the stiff placement of herself before the lights and camera. From Connecticut.

I was to sit many times and look at that picture and reread the address on the back and try to call up from my dim and buried years some recollection that would make more solid my own childhood.

Like the heroes of many Western dime novels who appear for the first time full grown, riding in from nowhere with no past, I had started life suddenly, though not full grown, at the age of seven . . . or was it six ? . . . and the subsequent years with the Andersons had virtually erased any memory I had ever had of what had gone on before I was sent out here to live with them.

I knew I had come west on an Orphan Train through New York City, courtesy of the New England Children's Aid Society. Mr. Anderson reminded me of that often enough.

"You forget who you were," he'd say. "You're here now and for good. You start here: you're an Anderson."

I had since read about it. There had been other children on many trains, most of them older than I was, boys and girls, all called "orphans." Some of them actually were. They had been gathered up from the streets and sidewalks, curbs and alleys of Connecticut, New Jersey, and New York and placed out—sometimes sold—west, lined up on station platforms or town halls and claimed by families who peered at the auction line of skinny arms and faces and made their selection, people who had responded to flyers offering children to families who needed them . . . or who needed workers. It was a very tempting situation for farmers on large plots of land.

For some of the children, it was salvation from a terrible and hungry life on the streets; others were merely a profit for stealthy human vultures. All the words sounded the same; all the speeches were for the good.

As I later went back through it all, it was hard to tell the genuinely concerned from the liars. Either way, children were tagged and shipped west, farm couples got their new sons and daughters from a railroad car, and totally different lives began.

I felt that I hadn't been from New York, for Connecticut made such a strange and hollow echo. I was one of the labeled children, classified as an orphan by the white tag tied to my jacket button, shipped by train to, it turned out, the Anderson family in Brewster, Ohio, and from that day forward entirely as separated from my own life and any recollections of my true family as if they had never existed.

I tell this now with much hindsight added, for when I took Cully back to his father's farm and found the picture of his lost mother, I did not know or remember my own past in any detail. I knew only that the address on the back of the picture stirred deep memories that were to swirl into my mind again and again until I felt driven to discover as much as possible about my own early years.

We drove silently back to my house, our house now.

CHAPTER 8

Cully

Doc says I have to go to school. I had been, sometimes, when we were in Ohio and a little now and again at the farm, but not regular. Nobody kept track of grades, so I just was fitted in by the teacher. It is that way this time, too.

The school is a small white building with a steep black roof. Outside is a whitewashed flag pole and a rusty green water pump on one side, and two whitewashed outhouses on the other. The playground is just open dirt in front, not like the grassy area at my last school. At the front of the building is a concrete slab and seven wooden steps that were painted gray once but are pretty worn down, and at the top of the steps is a big open space, like a built-in porch, with a door going off to each side. Once boys had to go in one side and girls in the other, but only one of the doors is used now. The other side is a storeroom.

The door leads into a coatroom where there's a white water tank we fill from the pump. The tank has a spigot at the bottom. The teacher, Miss Carty, makes up a list of who's to get the water or put up the flag or bring up wood from the cellar. If you're bad, you name gets added on again.

She has a yellow chart with our names on in a column, and across the page are columns for the days. If you are bad, she says, "Go give yourself a check!" in a mean voice, and we go to the chart and find our name and make a check under the right day. Three checks in one week and you get your hair pulled and have to stay late.

Inside, the school is one, high, open room with a big, black-iron wood stove with a black pipe running up into the wall. There are three tall windows on each wall of the room and two on one end, one on each side of the chimney.

But the windows start up at about my head, so we can't see out of their huge panes unless we stand up on our toes. There's also an old piano, and the music teacher comes once every month to teach us songs.

We have four groups in the room, and not everybody is the same age. My group was called grade 4, and I always sit next to Bobby who's in 4th grade for the second year. He's a nice boy. It's only about six people in all, just like the other grades. Some of the other kids were in their groups last year, too, and know the books.

I walk to school. The first day, Doc takes me, but I don't stay, and when he gets home from stopping to see about a sick horse, I am already back home in my room with Beans. He puts me back in his car, though, and drives me right back to the school, and Miss Carty has me sit with the older group. I don't think she even knows I was gone.

I know to read and count and make my cursive letters. We learn about the United States and all the states and their capitals. I am the first one that can spell Louisiana and Connecticut right. When we need to go to the outhouse, we must go to the blackboard by the door and write our initials in a box drawn along a crack in the lower corner of the blackboard so Miss Carty will know who's out of the room and that two people are not out at the same time. If you stay too long, she sends someone out to tell you to hurry up and get back inside.

After school we get wood from the cellar, putting it beside the stove, or stack it down there where the cart has dumped it outside by the window. Sometimes in winter it's too cold and we don't go to school.

Sometimes it's cold in school and our lunches freeze out in the entry.

At recess we play games on the dirt playground where there's a see-saw, or we throw a ball over the roof and shout "Hally, hally over!" and wait to see if somebody on the other side caught the ball and is running around to try to tag us. Then Miss Carty rings a big bell and we go back in.

It isn't always nice at school.

Once, Bobby told me to look out. He said he had heard something. So as soon as 3 o'clock came, I asked Miss Carty and said I had to go right home because Doc wanted to go somewhere. She said I didn't have to stack wood that day but could do it tomorrow. I think she could tell I was scared.

I ran across the room, through the coat room, and down the wooden steps. I don't remember running through the yard or past the tree where a couple of bikes were parked, but I must have. I ran out onto the hard, brown road toward Doc's. Each time I turned to look back, the schoolhouse was hidden a little more, and soon I couldn't see it. Just corn fields on each side.

Then I found I'd forgotten my book ! Doc always wanted me to bring my book home so's he could work with me some. The fear I had swelling in my stomach pushed up into my throat.

When I got back to the schoolhouse, I snuck along the high white side of the building, so close that I rubbed some of the dusty paint off onto my jacket. I could hear the guys down cellar stacking wood, but nobody was in the yard or the entry. My book was way across at my desk, but Miss Carty was in the storeroom and couldn't see me. The floor made so much noise. I grabbed my book but I dropped it, and the cover hit the floor open and bent a little on one corner. She wouldn't like that.

I ran back out through the yard and past the bikes. Henry's small bike was gone. So was Frankie's old one. They must have skipped out on the wood again. I hurried up the dirt road between the high crisp corn stalks. They rustled in the light wind, and some animal chirped and darted away as I went past Mr. Malkowski's place.

There were wobbly bicycle tracks in the road's soft dirt.

Then there was a strange noise. It was supposed to sound like wolves howling, but it wasn't. It came from the corn field beside me and kept getting louder and moving along with me. The big hollow in my stomach came back, but I didn't cry. I didn't dare. Instead, I walked real soft in hopes that I could sneak past while they were hiding, but right away there was a pathway into the cornfield and they could see where I was.

Henry jumped up, came out into the road, and walked backwards right in front of me, his face almost touching mine and his big belt buckle sometimes hitting mine. He had his black highcuts on. Frankie walked right behind me. He was taller than Henry, but Henry was the leader.

Nobody said anything. Henry had his arms folded across his chest and his scout knife swinging from his belt, and every now and then he would bump me with his chest and arms. He just stared at me. I couldn't stare back.

Then, without knowing why I did it, I clenched my fists. I couldn't help it, even if it was wrong. Right away Henry saw it and stopped, making me stop, too, with Frankie real close behind me.

"Fists, eh?" he said. "What're you going to do?"

I couldn't say anything, I was so afraid of him. Sometimes he was the greatest guy and we played together at recess and sat next to each other in 4th grade, and then he could do something like this. I started to go off to the side, but he moved over and I had to stop.

"Let me go home, Henry. Doc is waiting for me." I stopped and then said, "I like you."

"I don't like you," he said. "Never did, never will. What should we do to him?" he asked Frankie, talking past my shoulder. Frankie pushed me hard, so I bumped into Henry.

"Who you bumpin'?" Henry snarled, and he slapped the book out of my hand so that it skittered across the road. Then he shoved me back harder into

Frankie. Frankie punched my back and I felt my knees just give up, and I knelt down between them. I started to cry, no matter how hard I tried not to.

I hunched there, and they stood over me, saying what they were going to do now. "You shouldn't have tried that," Henry said, real soft and harsh, and they moved in closer, their legs pressing against me, and they slapped my head. I hardly remember the kicks.

I heard a dog bark, and looking past Henry's legs I could see Beans running towards me. I yelled once to her really loud, "BEANS, go back! Run!" and Henry kicked me in the side. He turned around and laughed, and Frankie laughed, and then Frankie let out a shrill, high whistle. From somewhere in the cornfield, his big, mean gray-brown hound dog trotted out between the stalks, toward us.

"Sic 'im !" Frankie shouted, pointing at Beans, and the hound broke toward Beans, his toenails scraping on the hard dirt road and pebbles flying backward.

"Run, Beans, run !" I screamed. "Run !" I was more scared than ever. I knew what Frankie's hound could do because I had seen him turned loose on some chickens once. The dogs raced down the road out of sight, and we just waited. Then Frankie whistled again and soon the hound came back, panting.

They stood and laughed, and I scrambled up, dashed over to pick up the scratched book, and ran, stumbling, tears blurring my eyes so that I could hardly see the road. They didn't follow. They just yelled things and laughed.

Beans was waiting for me after the second rise, still panting. She must have somehow outrun the hound. She wagged her tail and we both felt very lonely. I kneeled down by her. The road was hard but I didn't care. I put my arms around her. I held her as tightly as I could, and she just sat there and never moved until we started home when the air was cooler and very still.

She was alone, too, in spite of all my friendship.

And I knew it wasn't over.

CHAPTER 9

Doc

Cully came home very quiet. I could see that he'd been crying, but he didn't answer my question about "what's the matter?" Instead, he poked around things I had in my workshop, held one of the scalpels and twisted it back and forth in his fingers.

When he had settled a bit, he said, "How'd you know you wanted to be a veterinarian? D' you always know?"

It should have been an easy question with a direct answer. But I took a round-about way to the answer and started with a story I had told to only one other person.

"That's a long story. Really want to hear it?"

"Yeah," he said, settling quietly on a wooden crate in a corner, perched somewhere between his own thoughts and my explanation.

"It started when I was a boy at the Anderson farm. There was a story I loved, a legend about a boy who grew to become King Arthur. But what always interested me most, even from the time I was still young and Mrs. Anderson told me the tale for the first time, was his pet bird. He was like a pet crow I had once." The word caught his attention and he looked up, his face changing into a small smile.

"I always saw that bird as a hawk, not a falcon as some of the versions I read later had it. It was a sleek brown-black hawk, sharp eyes and talons, graceful flight, regal head.

"There were times when the visions I had of that hawk, spiraling up into the clouds, were enough to make me think I could fly. In my imagination I could when I was a boy. I even could do it in dreams, and that was the most real of all. Somehow I could will it; I'd just hold myself still and tense, even holding my breath some of the time, and I'd lift myself a few feet off the ground and start to glide along, and I could stay in the air as long as I concentrated and held myself just so."

"I've done that!" Cully exclaimed.

"I wasn't standing when I flew; I was sitting, with my legs in a natural sitting position and my feet down. But I could control the slow and gentle flight and sail across the land from several feet up. It was a glorious, free feeling, passing above roads, fields of corn, rivers. It never lasted very long, that dream, but every second of it was enchantment.

"I was even more awestruck when thinking of the hawk, wheeling higher and higher, invisibly tied to a point of earth by a raised, gloved hand, pulled back down by the apparently undeniable gravity of the boy's shrill whistle.

"Then one day in my dream, the hawk soared above the clouds without restraint, climbed through the crisp and blue-white vapors until, feeling a sun no one had ever seen before, he looked beneath him at the green and brown circle of earth reaching out in each direction, a roundness so intense and final that he blinked to be sure that this was sight and not another of his own dreams of height.

"The still earth reached far, all around, but ceased. And as he glided through the singing wind, its chill unnoticed now within the easy rhythm of his elevated flight, he saw the amazing sight: complete horizon everywhere, a darkened, solid ring surrounded by light, from silent gray on one side to brightest glaring whiteness on the other, a perfect circle sealed and mounted in the boundlessness of air.

"It was his moment of flawless joy, an instant never known before by bird or man or even mythic beast: the top of sky, the highest world, the silent passage beyond all that creatures knew.

"I always held the hawk in a suspended glory after that, even when the story started over and he was back in the midnight of blindfolded darkness to wait for freedom's chance again. Then, at last, I let him free and he was lost from sight, when I had disappeared beneath his view as but the first of the shrinking specks to vanish as he rose and rose, confined only by the unseen edges of space itself, to view again the all-horizoned world in soaring, solitary, and majestic rule.

"When I was about sixteen, Mrs. Anderson gave me a book and I read a passage by Thoreau, a person solitary and composed, compassionate and austere. He, too, had thought of hawks in <u>Walden</u>:

> *I observed a very slight and graceful hawk . . . . It appeared to have*
> *no companion in the universe. Where was the parent which hatched it,*

44

its kindred and its father in the heavens? The tenant of the air, it seemed related to the earth but by an egg hatched some time in the crevice of a crag.

"The first real hawk of my life was one without control of any aspect of its fate. It was an early August day that same year, sixteen. I watched him from my upstairs bedroom window, wheeling in large circles above our field. I'd guess he was a tired old hawk, floating way up in the sky next to God. Probably scared of people. But he must have had a pain in him for some food, so he floated down easy, circling, looking. Probably some folks saw him like that and thought how nice and free and smooth he looked; probably some folks did not notice him at all. Didn't hear the shotgun. Didn't see the feathers tear loose when the hot needles stung his chest and made him sick and dizzy, the earth churning up to meet him.

"Mr. Anderson stood in his front yard, gun held in both hands, and watched the hawk fall. There was only one thing in that old man's mind then: find that hawk and make sure he was killed. He called the dogs to come, and he limped fast out of the yard and up the dirt road toward the burning field, jamming a new shell in as he went toward where the brown, awkward, plummeting bird had fallen.

"Mrs. Anderson came to the back door and called something at him, but he didn't hear or didn't want to hear. He had a victory right there in front of him and no woman was going to take that away. He was already half-way across the pasture, toward the corn field. It was his kill and it would be a sure one. I ran after him and he half-turned and called, 'Keep back!' I did not obey.

"The hawk lay between rows of corn, its hot, dusty body rising and falling. When it heard the dogs, I imagine that it didn't want to live any more. Its breast must have pained more; its broken wing hurt twice as much. It tried to stop breathing, but it couldn't. It just kept panting, the warm, wet breaths bursting from inside it.

"Its head was turned a little by a sudden breeze, and it saw the dog bounding up the row. Its broken wing fluffed in the chilly wind and looked ugly, the detailed and exquisite feathers in disarray. Its throat was thick. The wind blew again, and the wing, bent awkwardly, fluffed a little more.

"The dog mouthed and carried the drooping body right past the old man, over to me. I held it, then took it back to my room, not to the pleasure of Mr. Anderson. I remember being quiet for a long time, even through supper. At first I had wanted to give it a grave, as one would a pet, but then I knew I wanted even more to see, to spy into the artistic, fine mechanisms that let this creature live as one who used the wind with balance, grace, and trust.

45

"It was my first dissection, done with a broken jack-knife and a pair of tweezers. Especially the wing structure was a fascination, the tiny, powerful arrangement of light bones and feathers that created flight.

In the end, the body did receive a grave. But the good wing remained with me, stared at in the frail light of my room, gently felt and moved in its half-hingelike motion until each part became a memorized link to every other part, each bone as clear in its placement as if I had designed the wing myself. And finally—the only remnants saved as symbols of my search—the longest feathers, once able to control the faintest or strongest currents of the sky.

"And that started it, I think. That was the beginning."

So when Cully trudged in late from school that day with Beans and with tear-streaked eyes and found me out in the barn and stood very close, I listened to his silence. When he asked about my work, I told him all I knew of the royal hawk, of imaginary flying, of my dream hawk's seeing the ends of space, of my first held hawk, of Henry Thoreau.

It was the first of talks about the past that eventually opened our way to the future. And I gave Cully one of the feathers to keep, remembering all the winds that all of us had known.

"Come on," I said to him. "We've got to go over to Hardesty's and check on those calves."

He came with me, as he always did, and he was quiet and thinking as we traveled. We had to stop and wait at the grade crossing south of Weed as a west-bound freight puffed across the plains, its rhythms steady and endlessly repeated as it clack-clacked over the rail connection just in front of us.

When it had passed, the bell stopped, the blinking lights went dark, and the gate rose again. Far to our right the red caboose got smaller and smaller in the silence of the land.

Cully said, "One hundred and fourteen."

THIRTY YEARS EARLIER . . . I

The Orphan Train

Part 1

The rhythmic rocking and bumping of the train finally put him to sleep. He had thought that he would never sleep again, but the regular sound, the darkness of the car, and the cup of milk had relaxed him at last. Once he woke in the night not remembering where he was, and was terrified of the motion and the sound, of a series of lights flashing past the window. It seemed that his own bedroom was moving, dashing violently somewhere into the darkness with a rattling rhythm and sudden bursts of light.

He remained quiet as he had always been taught to do, but terror filled his chest, and he stared into the long tunnel of darkness that was his room until he saw a person in a dark coat with buttons that shone when a flashing light went by. Slowly his eyes adjusted to the darkness; slowly he remembered the sounds; slowly he knew where he was and was now only bewildered, not terrified. The conductor walked carefully down the aisle, tucking the thin blankets around the sleeping children, speaking gently to any who were awake. "There's a good boy now. Just curl up comfortable. Having a hard time getting to sleep, are you? That's all right. Why don't you watch the stars outside the window."

He shifted his eyes and looked out the window as the conductor went past, seeing the uniformed reflection and no stars. From somewhere ahead, a distant whistle . . . looong, looong, short, looong. A crossing. Then only the clacking rhythm and the slight swaying again. And the darkness.

Finally, sleep.

He was one of the first to wake. A huge, bright, blazing sun rose from the left, and as they clattered past the backs of some buildings, all the little windows showed flames and he was mesmerized in watching them. Every building in this city was on fire it seemed, and no one even noticed. Men in the alley worked at unloading a cart; others walked slowly along carrying their lunch pails. Fire! He sprang to his knees, his face against the thick, filmy window, and tried to stare through the rushing small windows of all the flaming buildings to see the fire that was inside, his hands spread flat and pressed hard against the railway car window and his heart battering his breath into short, open-mouthed bursts of frightened air. "Fire!" he heard his heart shout. "Fire!" as tears rolled down his cheeks and cut small rivers into the window's film.

The train swung around a curve. By pressing his cheek against the window, he could see the black, puffing engine far ahead and many of the cars which led back to his, a long dark-green parade of passenger cars moving slowly along the turn underneath a spreading tunnel of black smoke.

On the ground and then splashed suddenly across buildings, the train's dark silhouette seemed to flow with the surfaces, flat against buildings then back on the ground, always moving, racketing along fences and dipping suddenly into streets, then up again on the sides of buildings. The rushing shadow narrowed and narrowed, sliding closer to the moving train, joining the track bed almost as one, uniting with the cars as they headed directly away from the rising sun. And the fires in all the windows went out.

The seat was reddish, gentle and fuzzy like velvet almost, and he softened his worries by rubbing his hands over it again and again, back and forth, maybe thousands of times, absorbing the soft feel and lulled by its closeness. The back of the seat was far above his head, and once yesterday he had kneeled on the seat and looked back into the car and then toward the front, and here and there he saw a child's head and remembered that in some of the other seats, too, there were children.

The older ones were tall enough to see without kneeling. Others, younger and smaller like him, could only guess at what lay beyond the dark wall of the seat ahead. When he moved to the inside edge of the seat, leaned up over the arm rest, and peered down the narrow aisle, he saw small feet, some with shoes, small hands, here and there an arm in motion. Once he saw a face looking back at him, and equally startled, he and it pulled back suddenly as if doing something forbidden. He heard their voices sometimes, but never loud, never like many children together, and he wondered where they were going.

He sat back on the seat and watched as the buildings grew smaller, then there were houses and back yards with sheds and chicken coops, then only a few, then just the land again. They were moving into a vastness he had never known, and even the brilliance of the rising sun could not make it golden.

Sometimes the small passengers crowded to one side or the other when someone called "Look!" Excited and jabbering, the city children rushed to the window and climbed on each other to see. Then, almost without speaking, they stared at apple trees, a small-town carnival, horses in a field, geese on a pond; craning their necks when the sight raced past, watching it until they could see it no longer, then drifting back to their own seats and exclaiming over what they had just seen.

Part 2

The first day had been nightmarish for him. Two of the older boys were wild and eventually fought, causing a large man in a brown suit to come in and force them apart, then tie each to his seat. He shouted at them and they shouted back, and in no time one had undone the ropes which held his arms down and had fled to the back of the car, hitting every child he could reach as he ran past, whacking heads and arms, screaming bad language and once stopping to try to rip a seat back from its frame.

He crashed through the car's rear doorway with a sudden metallic explosion and burst into the next car, thumping people and raging so loudly that even his motions were like cries echoing back through the cars. Then he disappeared into the next car, arms flailing as the children strained over their seats to watch.

A frightening rumor worked its way back several hours later that, now pursued by the man in brown and a conductor with a gun, he had tried to climb into the caboose and had been locked out. So he climbed over the grilled gate which kept passengers from the side landings, leaned out with his hair raggedly blowing in the wind of the rushing train, and leaped off to be free.

Word passed excitedly forward that the boy had jumped just as the train passed a switch, and the vertical post of the black switch lever had smashed his head and broken his neck, and those who could see back down the tracks said that he hung there like a scarecrow, growing ever smaller as the train left him behind.

The boy in the next seat back had asked the conductor later if the story were true, but the conductor had said, "No, of course not. That didn't happen." So they knew it was true.

That first night, he did not eat. The sounds of the night were the patter of the wheels on the rails, the strange and distant whistle of the train, and the crying of children. Everywhere, it seemed to him, he heard sobbing, small sobbing of little voices being carried far into the land. He knew that sisters sometimes were allowed to sit together, but they were in another car. This held only boys, and he was alone in his high seat, a small thin leaf in a big red cup, silent in this frightening newness, imagining monsters and evil men, knowing no trust at all in the lady's words that he was being taken "to a good home with a kind family and would like it there."

So the first night had passed without sleep, without food, without going to the bathroom because he did not know where it was. One little boy wet his pants and the seat, and the conductor saw it and stomped down the aisle and out of the car only to return with the man in brown who stripped the child's pants off, spanked the boy and scolded him and made him sit naked until they could dry his pants and return them to him. When he whimpered that he wanted to go home, he received the same stern message that anyone heard if they asked about home: home had been bad, home no longer existed, they were going to a new home.

Only the woman seemed to try to soothe the children, talking to them gently, saying it would be all right. She said all the children before had felt the same way at first and then later liked their new lives. She said that there wasn't much farther to go and that good people were waiting to take them into their families. Sometimes, if she saw that a child was especially distressed, she sat down with that child and spoke softly and held its hand. The child calmed then, stopped crying, even took the crackers the woman offered. But when she rose and left, the child sat still and straight, tears running down its cheeks, for it understood now that there never would be any going back.

By the third day, the children had become used to the pattern: they knew where the bathroom was at the end of the car, they ate the thin food which was brought to them, and they even talked to each other a little bit. Their remarkably similar stories were of little interest to each other, and so they boasted of the things they used to be able to do at home, of the games they played, of the climbing they had done or the tricks they had played on grownups.

Some were, even at less than ten years of age, remarkably inventive story tellers, and their tales pulled groups of children toward them, sitting, standing, perched on seat arm-rests, kneeling in the aisle to hear the tales the small tellers would weave. It was a wondrous circle that these stories created, enthralling the listeners for miles and miles which dragged them ever further from home. But while the story was on, that was forgotten: a new world existed, sometimes even with laughter, and even the youngest felt warmer and safe.

There also developed in many a sense of protectiveness, of caring, as young boys and girls became parents in the train to children hardly three or four years younger than themselves, making the travel less lonely and the darkness less separating. These slightly older ones knew from their own *isolated backgrounds in the city alleys and dead ends what it was to need, and they somehow saw the younger ones as their own to tend and soothe and protect within the dark windowed walls of the moving train car. It was an imitation of love, perhaps, but it was better than nights of sobbing and desperately lonely children, and everyone began to accept the familiness of the others in the car and, from that, gain confidence that everything was going to be all right because they were together.*

The woman came to the car again in mid-morning and told them that it was not much longer now. Then she started to get them ready. They all had to put on the clothes which she brought into the car, used clothes but still new to them after the smells of the days of travel, and exciting to put on. She made them wash their faces and hands, and then she combed the hair of the oldest boys and someone fixed up the hair of the girls with red barrettes, showing them in a little hand mirror just how nice they looked. Then she had the older ones help wash and dress and comb and brush the younger ones, readying them all for some grand moment they did not yet understand, reading to them again as their attention wavered and then disappeared as they sensed and then knew that the train was slowing to a stop.

She could not control them then, their excitement was so grand to see. "Remember," she admonished them, "remember that you are to stand beside the train in a row, tallest at the end nearest the engine." She had gone over this with them twice, but she was never sure that every child listened. Some simply seemed unable to listen, as if paying attention to directions was such a foreign thing to them that they simply vanished into a mind-wandering blankness and heard nothing. But she knew that the others, whom she tended to call "the good ones," would herd the confused ones into line fairly well and the selection process could begin. If they were lucky, the train would be empty after three or four stops, and they could start home again. The next load was not due for nearly three months.

"This will be just a short stop," she said. "Just one hour, so we won't go to the church. We'll just line up on the station platform and some of you will meet your new families there. If you do not get placed here, don't worry. There are several more stops further west, and lots more chances."

As the train began to slow, the children rushed to the windows on the station side of the car, watching to see what people were there to meet the train, only the older ones truly understanding that they might be selected to go home with someone and start a new life in whatever state and whatever town this was. They were not opposed to the idea. They were not the ones who had sobbed at night; they were children for whom home had meant hardship, beatings, little food, sickness, many people cramped into one or two rooms, filth. Some would have been lucky to have had even that, for they were the ones called "street Arabs," waifs of the garbage alleys, pirating life from fruit vendors and open markets, stealing survival daily, aging into the craggy-faced teenagers who seldom saw twenty. For them, even the thin food on the train and the clean used clothes had been heaven. For them, living in a house, any house, would be so wonderful and positive that they would endure hard work simply not to have to go back. For them, an adult's voice that was not a policeman's or a magistrate's would be an angelic sound of safety and hope.

They crowded now, those who knew, up against the filmy windows as the train slowed into its puffing entrance to the station, and they eagerly scanned the people on the platform in search of someone who might choose them and take them to a new beginning.

Part 3

The posters had been up for more than two weeks, placed by an advance agent who knew that the post office, the grocery store, church bulletin boards, the drug store (if there was one), and the saloon were the best places to advertise the coming of the Orphan Train. "Homes for Good Children Wanted."

The message was simple and clear. Come to see the children who were available for adoption; talk to them, determine their age and strength and health, have them walk about like horses up for auction; select or not as you saw fit. If you chose one, you paid the fee to the person at the table, registering name, address, child's name, and other basic data. If within two months the match did not work out, you could notify the agency and the child would be taken back at the next visit of the Orphan Train and reentered into the available pool, all money refunded.

In fact, the agreement did not work that way. Any mismatches generally were disregarded by the adopting family unless the child seemed to be beyond control. Even then, there was some doubt when, if ever, the train would return, and even less chance of receiving a refund. In plain truth, once selected, selected for life.

Mrs. Anderson knew all this. She had spoken with others who had adopted a child from the train two months ago down in Belle Haven. When she saw the posters in Brewster, she told her husband who, despite misgivings, knew that another hand on the farm would be useful. Mrs. Anderson's motives were quite different. Both her children had died in infancy. Here, she knew, was a chance to select a young child whom she could raise properly, someone who desperately needed a good family, someone who had no home. Her goal was to have a true child of her own. That would mean taking a young one, of course. Mr. Anderson would not like that. But it would give her the chance to raise the child properly, not have to break a decade's worth of bad habits. She sat for the interview with the local Placement Committee and was accepted.

She stood back against the station wall growing more and more nervous as the train sounds approached from the east, still at least a half-mile away, squeezing and crushing the money in her pocket in her anxious moments of final decision whether to go through with this or not.

As the train pumped black smoke into the sky and moved up the wavering tracks to the Brewster station, people left their cars and trucks and wagons, moving toward the platform, curious, unsure. These were farmers who knew a good cow or hog when they saw one, knew how to feel a horse's chest and legs and look at the teeth, knew a good ear of corn and the color of fine wheat ready for harvest. But they did not know how to take the measure of a strange child who would stay in their lives for several years. Chest? Teeth? Legs? Color? Did you feel the muscles, and if so, what should you expect? These were city kids. Who could tell which ones would adapt to the farm life? Should we talk to them? Ask them . . . what? They had been deloused, the poster said, and were certified to be "healthy and free of disease."

Mrs. Anderson wished she had brought her neighbor, Helen Majorson, to help her choose and decide. Something which had seemed so simple and free from complications now seemed to her nearly an impossibility. She was going to pick out one child from among the nearly one hundred on the train, and it had to be the right one or Mr. Anderson would rage and be a taciturn ogre to live with. She moved a step toward the train, now nearly stopped, not quite knowing where to stand or how to begin her search. Others moved forward, too, and then paused as if awaiting instructions.

From the train—its dark and powerful engine now one hundred feet further down the tracks puffing silver clouds from its sides and just a thin black smoke from the smokestack—stepped a middle-aged man in a brown suit, his jacket open and a gold watch fob strung across his vest front. He scanned the people waiting on the platform, his face serious and official, his manner important, almost haughty.

"Ladies and gentlemen," he started. Most in the crowd gave him their attention, but some had not heard him and he was irritated. He reached back onto the car's landing and picked up a piece of metal pipe, turned back to the crowd for a minute, and then whanged the pipe against the hard rails of the car's steps. The sound was that of a blacksmith hammering heated iron into a shape on an anvil, and the crowd respected the noise and became still.

"Ladies and gentlemen," he said again and paused. "That's better. Thank you for coming to help us aid the poor children of the cities of the East. They are good children but they are orphans. They need good homes. They are eager to become useful and hard-working members of your families.

"Please follow my instructions carefully. We want everyone to have a chance to see and select from all the children. Therefore, remain orderly and everyone will have a good opportunity to make their selections. Do not approach the children until they are all in place and I give the indication that you may begin.

"Once you have made your selection, bring the child to the table set up in the station, and there I will collect the fee and take the necessary information, after which I will give you a certificate officially naming you as the adoptive parents of the child. After that, you may head home. The train will leave precisely in one hour, so you will need to have made your selection by then.

"In a minute I will ask the children to come forward and line up for your inspection. Please examine them carefully and then make your choice. Mrs. Palcher, my assistant"—and here the woman who had read stories leaned forward from the train-car platform and waved to the crowd—"will be with you and will help you in your selections.

"Now," he said, turning back toward Mrs. Palcher, "Let's have the children."

She had gotten them lined up fairly well within the cars, but now as they came hesitantly down the steps to stand beside the oil-smelling train cars, they had to do some blending so that the children from all the cars were arranged by height.

Down they came, stepping awkwardly or boldly, looking with trepidation or defiance or bashfulness at the farm-dressed adults looking at them. The mingling of sizes went on with Mrs. Palcher herding the older children into line and asking two of the girls to go to the other half and help the younger, shorter children to line up, each an arm's length apart. They did. Soon the line was complete, nervous shifting and unsure eyes, hands first in front then at the sides then in back, as the farm people looked from fifteen feet away and spoke in whispers and pointed at one or another.

Mrs. Anderson let her eyes move toward the shorter children. It would have to be a boy. Even if a girl seemed the best pick, Mr. Anderson would never tolerate a little girl in the house. She would hear endlessly for years about the missed opportunity to select a healthy and strong boy to help on the farm. "What'd you even go for if you were going to pick a girl?" he would say. "What good is a girl going to be?"

Her searching gaze fell finally on a boy who seemed to be about eight, a tall, thin boy with blond hair and long fingers. His white tag said in huge black printing that he was number 45 and that his name was Albert. She watched him for a few minutes, and when the brown-suited man said that they could approach the children, she started toward him, certain that he was the one she wanted even before she spoke to him.

As she neared Albert, other adults rushed across in front of her from both directions, and she felt almost as if she were in a human stampede. She was jostled a bit and realized that others, too, had their mind set on Albert. Before she got close enough to speak to him, someone else, a man, had taken Albert by the wrist and was leading him through the crowd, back into the station to the registration table.

Several children were being taken now, one by one. Sometimes couples but mostly a man or a woman alone would choose a child and start with him or her toward the arched entrance to the station building where, in an open area in front of the ticket seller's window, an oak table and chair had been set up for the payment of fees, the answering of questions, and the bestowal of the certificate of adoption.

Occasionally the child, especially one of the smaller girls, was picked up and carried just as a parent would hoist a favorite into the air and carry her facing forward through the crowd of people. There were smiles on many faces, although some were stern. Sometimes a child would resist, would tug backwards when a person took his arm, would start to scream and kick and bite and cry and force the adult to let go. Once or twice Mrs. Anderson heard an angry "Well, the hell with you then" as a struggling child was released. Once a child dashed back into the railway car and stayed there; once a child ran down the platform toward the engine, but that way was no escape; he was certain to be caught by the lacing arms of many adults who would not permit flight. The others were docile, well behaved, or, in Mrs. Palcher's word, "good."

Mrs. Anderson was perplexed now. Her chosen one had been taken. If she went home without a child, that, too, would bring on the wrath of Mr. Anderson. She decided to keep looking.

One whom she really liked was a sweet-looking girl with brown curls, probably seven or eight years old. She had a sparkling eye and a beautiful smile, and Mrs. Anderson almost went against Zeus's thunder and selected her. She did move closer to the little girl and saw that she was 78 Marcia and that she was, indeed, eight. What a lovely flower of springtime she would be . . . would have been . . . on their farm, she thought. "Good luck, pretty Marcia," she said softly to herself. "Good luck."

Her eyes rested finally on the small boy near the end of the line, a boy whose tag said he was Number 17 John. She approached him and stood a few feet in front of him, noticing his fine dark eyes and brown hair.

"John?" she said.

He did not respond.

"John?" He was alert and looking at everything that was going on further down the platform, but he did not seem to hear her. Was he deaf? "John?"

"He probably doesn't know you are calling to him. We don't know what his name really is," said Mrs. Palcher who had seen Mrs. Anderson's interest in the boy and had moved closer to assist her. Mrs. Anderson looked at her puzzled. "No," said Mrs. Palcher, "he would not tell us his name. He would not even speak to us at first, but even when he would talk to us, he would not tell us his name, so we called him John. Do you like him?"

"Yes, I do," said Mrs. Anderson. "John? Is that your real name? she asked. Mrs. Palcher stood beside her, a bit closer to the boy, and listened with benevolent interest.

"No," said the small boy.

"Well, my name is Mrs. Anderson. Will you tell me your real name, your first name, so I can call you properly?" asked Mrs. Anderson.

"No," he said, shaking his head, speaking almost sadly, as if he would like to have told her but was, for some reason, afraid to.

"I live on a big farm with many animals and wide fields. Would you like to live on a farm?"

"Yes," he said, and there seemed to be interest in his eyes and voice, even in that one word. It was a small voice, a shy voice, but it was firm in the way it spoke the word.

"Look at his hands," said Mrs. Palcher, gesturing with her open hand that the boy should turn his hands palm up for Mrs. Anderson to see.

"May I see your hands?" Mrs. Anderson asked, pleased when he so quickly lifted his arms out to her and held his hands out. What she saw surprised her, for these *were not the hands of a little city boy. The hands were lightly callused: he had done work. "Did you live on a farm?" she asked.*

"Yes," he said.

"How old are you?"

"Seven, almost." He said.

"Your tag says you are six. But you are seven 'almost'?" she said, and she smiled at him. "Will you tell me your name now?"

"No, ma'm," he said shyly.

"I think you would like living on our farm, John," she said. "Would you like to come home with me and help take care of the animals and help Mr. Anderson on the farm as you get older?" Mrs. Palcher beamed and nodded, as if cueing John as to what his answer should be.

He looked again at the people further down the platform. Some places in the line were empty now. He looked back at the dark train which smelled of hot grease, steam issuing from underneath with a sound like breathing, as if the train were alive and merely resting. "Yes," he said. "That would be okay."

"But your name is not John, is that right?"

He nodded.

"Would you mind if you and I and Mr. Anderson chose a new name for you that you would keep? Would that be all right? And we can give you our last name, Anderson, too, and you will be part of the family. Does that sound all right?"

"Yes," said young John, soon to be John no more, soon no more to be whoever he really was, as he would become an Anderson and live on the Anderson farm ten miles outside of Brewster, Ohio.

Mrs. Anderson shook Mrs. Palcher's hand, and the lady warmly hugged John and told him how lucky he was and what a good home he was going to. Mrs. Anderson thanked her and watched as John followed her into the station. She was pleased that she did not have to hold his arm to be sure that he would not dart away.

She paid the fee to the man in brown, filled out the name and address information, read the agreement and signed it, swearing that she would keep the child properly fed and in good health, would see that he got schooling; and she duly received a copy of something that purported to be an official certificate of adoption. She knew it wasn't. She knew that they did not know a thing about this boy who had been given the name John. She knew that she disliked the officious man in brown and felt almost as if she were rescuing John from an unholy person.

While she paid and signed, John watched the platform and saw that people had started to leave. Children who had not been picked were being directed back onto the train, and when they got inside many of them went to the windows and looked out at the emptying station platform, its wooden planks and concrete now decorated with discarded sheets of paper, name tags, tissues, and a stray sock. He heard the woman called Mrs. Palcher say loudly, "Eleven of them?" and the man in brown checked his list and nodded. "But it was a small town," he said. Then they boarded the train. He saw the engine do its many rapid puffs to break the friction of the heavy iron wheels on the tracks, and then it began an increasing and powerful rhythm of gigantic smoke puffs as it pulled away from the station with growing noise and speed. And as it went, small faces with flat noses looked back through the train's windows.

She turned, then, to the boy and said, "Our wagon is out back here. Let's go home and see the farm and introduce you to Mr. Anderson." She said it gaily, smilingly, but inside was quite worried at Anderson's reaction to seeing such a young boy. She looked again at John, soon to be given a new name, and he looked up at her with a clear, open look.

She had not anticipated the feel of her heart pushing against her throat at this moment as she and her new son walked to the wagon.

PART III

Passages

CHAPTER 10

Doc

Cully asked, one day, about my being a veterinarian. We were in the shed when it began, and I could hear his mumbling voice trying to read aloud the labels on some bottles and cans I had there.

He leaned back and his head around a corner. He looked at me at the work bench.

"What'er you doing?"

"Trying to modify the wiring in the hot cloth to make it fit a horse's upper leg, too."

"What're those?" he asked, as his body scuffled around the corner as if drawn by the strength of his gaze, and he pointed off to the side.

"Farrier's tools," I answered. "Never seen them before?"

"No. For what?"

"That's a farrier's stand, used to hold a horse's hoof when he's working on it. This one's called a buttress. It's used to clean the hooves of a horse. Here's a horse knife." He took it and ran his finger tips along it, sensing it to get to know it. "Here's a tool that repairs a horse's worn down teeth." He handled it the same way.

"Why do you still keep these old horseshoes? When we were at Mr. Kulba's barn, he did the same thing, had a pile of them there, never seemed to throw any horseshoes out. Why not?"

"I take it you don't believe in the good-luck theory of horseshoes."

"Not really. Besides, one or two would do for that."

I asked, "So why would you keep them? What reason might *you* have for saving something like that, assuming that it was no good for a horse any more."

He scratched his nose with his thumb and finger, ran the finger down the bridge, squinted. "It must be for something else," he said, "some other thing than horses."

"Such as?"

Long silence. Thinking. "It could hook two things together!"

"Like the barway of a fence, for example?"

He smiled. He was pleased to realize that just because an object was made for one purpose did not mean that it couldn't do something else. He looked over the rest, and the blacksmith tools, beyond the anvil and the top and bottom swages—fullers, hot punches, dividers, tongs, forging hammers—trying to look beyond their actual use, I think, and find some other way for them to be a help.

He was gone for a moment, then back again, gone and back, each time holding out a bottle of something and wanting to know its uses.

"'Doctor Daniels' Veterinary Medicine,' he read. "Does it work?"

"Read what it says," I told him.

"Wonder Worker Lotion—the most wonderful healer ever known for sprains, sores, or wounds, either new or old harness galls, cuts, sore shoulders, scratches . . . ." He stopped. "This cures *everything*. Does it?"

"Would you think so?"

"Don't see how it can. Are they all the same?"

"No. Some are cuts, some are soreness in the muscles."

"So how can it do both?"

"Maybe it can't. Maybe it can do one well and the other only a little. But it still might be good for both; maybe it's not 'the most wonderful healer' because that's just to help sell it. But it does help some ailments of the animals, and if it helps, then it's up to me to use it right."

He read another: "'Oster-cocus Liniment—nerve, bone muscle.'" He looked at me questioningly. I nodded and winked.

"Same," I said.

"'Hamamelis Triple Extract Kloudy Witch Hazel,'" he read. He no longer needed to question me. Now he was just enjoying the names.

"'Renovator Powder—a true conditioner for horses and cattle—a tonic and bloodmaker.' *Bloodmaker*? Is that true, Doc. Can it really make blood?"

"Not in the way you mean. What it does, or is supposed to do, is add iron and other strengtheners to the blood to make it stronger so the animal can fight off diseases as it heals. Read that next one." I smiled.

"'Physic Balls—colic, worms, congestion, constipation, indigestion, staggers, hidebound, dropsy, lymphangitis, founder, stoppage, spinal meningitis.' Wow!" he said, properly awestruck as if at his own feat of pronouncing all those big words. The one that interested him the most, though, was 'staggers.' Then he looked at 'famous dog remedies,' a bottle of eye wash, some 'distemper cure,' even some hoof dressing. "I could never remember all that," he said.

"Yes, you will. Once you start using them, you will understand that they help and get used to working with them. Some of them you could apply right now and do it right. Remember that the patient never asks you to read him the label."

"Is that how you got started? Reading labels? I know you went to the agriculture college some. You told me about the hawk. Will that ever happen to me?

"Yes, I bet it will, only you won't figure it out until later. Some day you'll be doing a job that works your hands but your mind is free, and you'll remember something that happened when you were young, and you'll understand that that was the start of it."

"Like your hawk?"

"Not just the hawk, although he was an important part of it, because he showed me not just bones and muscle and feathers, but also what a marvelous thing a creature is in the way it's put together. But there was a deeper kind of interest, a sympathy and a wondering, that always had me aimed this way, I think. It might have started back on a farm, once."

And, so, we sat on upturned pails, leaning against the shed wall, our backs against the cool shed and the sun softening our shirts and pant legs with warmth. He worked a small twig around as I spoke, telling him another story that gained a solid place in my memory only with this telling.

The tale seemed a fiction from an ancient time when such events were legend. It taught me that I was not so much a stranger to the land as once I'd thought; not solely educated to the life of nature's self or made into a caring man merely by books and desks and lectures. There had been a bond in it after all from many years ago on land now changed, I suppose, owned now by someone who would never know the stories of the woods: a tale which must exist forever or the truth will fade, too, into property, into results, and measurable boundaries. It happened when I was about twelve, about Cully's age.

The land was young yellow-green growth topping the hill and deep away from usual paths, and in its midst, for some unknown and never questioned reason, a small orchard had lived despite its planter passing on. The cow, Eppie, had not come in and everyone grew concerned. It was the third day and night, and Eppie, who usually wandered in from the pasture without a call, had not been seen; the barn door had been left open in the dark, as everyone believed that Eppie would come in, sometime, by instinct or hunger or just the deep embedded sense of coming home.

But when the fourth evening came and the cow was still not back, Mr. Anderson sent me, apparently without much hope, to search the upland orchard area while others went their various assigned routes into the brush and woods and pasture corners.

I had a light, a lantern, but the old timber trail was clear enough in the gleam of the large and dashing moon. The path led upward, not so fast as to be tiring, yet still a rising that slanted across side hills and switched back into the upper woods and crossed again through brush and old bushed clearings, now become again the starting ground for newer growths of maple, pine, oak, and hemlock.

"Listen for her bell," someone had said. And still I heard no bell at all. Sometimes a bird, an owl, a distant calling not aware of me, but never anything that told me "cow."

The woods grew taller and the night seemed darker now, a subtle, deepening shade that fades so slowly that one is nearly lost within its shadow before remembering to be wary.

Avoid the stinging branches, the impossible horizontal cobwebs strung yards across the path, the stones that wrench the ankles, the vines that grow in sudden snares to trip such foolish, wandering feet as mine. And still no bell.

The hill this time was not so tall, yet always it was filled with distance and with wonder, and from a clearing near the top, the climber could look back and down and see the farmhouse lights, tiny and distant, another world which must be centuries away. The gulf of night between me and the house was solid and immense, a black sheet of depth without detail or form or substance. It was merely there, separating me from the warmth and safety of the house.

I stumbled on amidst the brush and trees, then jarred to a frozen halt at something standing in my shade-dark way, something ominously immense and solid just beyond clear sight yet looking at me steadily, breathing loudly without motion. I stopped and steadied, my trembling, leaden arm almost unable to hold the lantern out to see. A smaller figure to the side crashed suddenly and scared me into a chilling fear.

It was a calf. Eppie had had a calf. She had stayed up here by the orchard to tend to it, eating the grasses and the leaves and fruit, feeding her calf until it strengthened itself and could return.

"Eppie," I said, my breath a relief in the night as fear released and welcome joy swarmed in. "Eppie, good Eppie!" I praised, and truly loved her stand against my brusque and crashing entrance on her secret birthing place.

I then must have decided that the calf had to return home, but its young legs were not a match for any ragged hillside path, and I was not about to stay the night out in the sudden, grasping wilderness.

After stroking Eppie's cool moist nose and high-ribbed side, and gradually working my way along her to the sometimes-staggering calf, feeling her head turning, I put the lantern on a rock and smoothed my hands along the calf's sides and legs and neck and head, checking its perfection, enjoying the smell and softness of such a helpless child of the woods. After more stroking of Eppie, who had turned to watch my motions with special and silent concern, and after many gentle words to both and quiet tinklings of Eppie's bell, I blew out the lantern, stood beside the calf, and, surrounding its legs with both my arms, ducked my head under its belly and lifted, not sure I could do it, heavier even than I had guessed, its short, soft coat snug around my neck. Eppie moved to me, nosing my intentions and waited, apparently satisfied.

We crossed to the orchard's edge and started down the moon-painted path, the guiding farmhouse lights gleaming in the tiny distance. Every step I took was carefully measured now for both of us, and right behind, her nose sometimes bumping my back, Eppie trailed me and her silent calf, its calmness almost strange. Now I heard the cow—its hoofs, its breathing, and its bell—for every step and shift sent forth the ringing of the celebration as we descended to the safety of the barn's calf pen.

The trip back down seemed miles of aching arms and shoulders until we hit level ground and I set the calf down to walk, but what a joyous surprise we had, Eppie and I, for the rest back at the barn. The large signal bell was unneeded to call the others in from their searches: I was the last one back.

They did not believe me: the calf was too heavy for me to have carried, they said.

It was the last calf born on that farm. Two weeks later, Mr. Anderson had a seizure, and two months after that he died, having not spoken to me again after his denial of my story.

Cully still sat, the shadows of the shed now angling across his legs so that only his shoes were in sunlight. He turned.

"What did Mr. Anderson die of?" he asked.

"Stroke," I think. "When it first hit him it took away his speech and his right side. After that, he just sat and looked blankly across the room as Mrs. Anderson tried her best to care for him. But it was like caring for a statue almost. He never spoke, never moved. Then he died."

"Did you stay there then? After that?"

"Yes. Mrs. Anderson and I worked the farm, and she was able to hire a young man from a near-by family to do much of the work when I was in school. But you're right. I know what you mean. Things began to change. It's hard to separate the years now, but I went on to a high school on a bus each day, and then to college, and after she died, too, I didn't go back but just kept going on."

"Did Eppie stay on the farm?"

"Yes she did. She lived there the rest of her life, and we were very sorry when she grew ill and the veterinarian came and said that there was nothing we could do."

"Is she there still?"

"Yes. She's still there." I turned and smiled at him. I knew he'd ask that.

CHAPTER 11

Doc

The land in this part of southern Illinois had long since become used to me, but it took longer for people to become used to us. The men on the bench in front of the store seemed to pay no notice to us, just the customary nod, as we went into the store. But their look was different. Cully always went with me on my visits to farms, worked with me in my patch of a garden, tended the animals, helped in my small blacksmith shop or barn when that was needed, and began to learn some of the proper procedures for caring for sick, lame, or injured animals. He even grabbed hold and helped get the last Hardesty calf born when its mother was having a hard time.

He was a curious boy, an interested one, so it was almost strange that he spoke so little, as if he did not remember his father's death or that his aunt had deserted him. At least he never mentioned those things. Nor did he mention his mother. He was a lot like me.

None of my notices in the paper about having him with me brought a response: Aunt Clara was either out of range of my inquiries or simply did not want to have to take the boy on again. So now, with my goat and dog and chickens and cows, I had found a boy.

His quiet way made me realize that I, too, had not ever inquired about my past before the Andersons, had let the changes occur as if they were Fate and I could not affect the outcomes nor discover the causes. It was the beginning, I see now, of my own search.

Cully was stoic about some pain, such as when he fell out of the apple tree and landed on his back on the ground had the wind knocked out of him for a while. I know it scared him to lie there and be able to see and think but not be able to move. When he caught his breath after a few seconds, he got up and ran inside and stayed alone in his room until he had settled down again. Some things hurt him, but he never wanted me to see it. He was trying to be a man without letting himself be just a child first.

He was excellent with animals and quickly learned to tend the smaller ones, to ride a horse, to lead a cow properly, to milk it. He had a magic way with hogs, speaking to them and somehow getting them to stand and watch him as he fed them or walked through their pens, doing some things many grown men would have been hesitant to do, knowing that large hogs could be dangerous.

He gave the hogs names, usually characters from books we had been reading, or even authors' names, and after a while they seemed to respond to him as if they understood. He called one big one Shakespeare, and another that he didn't quite trust he named Macbeth. One mean sow was just Madame Defarge, and a twisty old grizzled-looking solitary boar was Scrooge. Our evening reading was having a useful result.

One evening that first winter, we were sitting at supper in the kitchen. The daylight had long since vanished. I had lighted the lamp and we ate the stew and the fresh bread Mrs. Bonner had brought over.

Cully seemed to draw with his spoon on the red-patterned oilcloth beside his plate before he asked, "What's a hawk do in winter time?"

"What does he eat, you mean?"

"No. Where's he stay when there's a blizzard?" The spoon stopped, its tip pointed at a little flower in the pattern.

"Well, if there's snow on the ground, his hunting job is probably made easier. During the spring, summer, and fall, little rodents and rabbits can blend in with the ground and bushes and grasses and be hard to spot. That's why he's got such sharp eyes. But in winter, if they come out to forage, they stand out pretty clearly against the snow, or even against the hard, bare ground, and he can wait patiently and then swoop down. He goes far, you know, he's not just over this field or that. He covers hundreds of miles if he wants to. And his eyesight is so keen that even a little trembling of a stick down there tells him that a mole or mouse is stirring about."

Suddenly, two shorts and a long on the wall phone interrupted us, my ring, and I pushed back and went to answer it. The black receiver was old and scarred, and its sound was a little scratchy now, but it was some people's only contact, calling through Central to someone on the line.

When I hung up, I wasn't sure what to say. I stayed there by the phone, turned and looked over at Cully at the table. "Mrs. Bailey," I said. "She needs help. She thinks something's wrong with Ben. You can stay here if you want."

But he lifted his chair back, snatched his jacket off the back of it, tugged it on, and came with me.

Margaret and Ben Bailey lived down the road about three-quarters of a mile, but we could short-cut there across the two or three fields in between. Cully had become so good at going cross-lots to places that some of his schoolmates called him "field mouse."

The Baileys were an old-looking couple in their fifties, land-hardened people who might come out a little ahead from year to year but who were simple and were satisfied just to come out even. We did not see them often, not for more than a "Hello" in passing since Cully had been with me.

The fields had close-cut stubble in them from the corn harvest, and the walk was more like a trek, heavy walking and cold air making us pant. Nevertheless, Cully went back to his questions.

"What's he do in a storm?" he asked, turning his face toward me at the same time trying not to let the freezing wind get at him.

"What do *you* do in a storm?" I asked him, not turning.

"I get inside and stay out of the wind and have a fire."

I laughed. A very practical answer. "Well, so does he. He finds a safe spot. He's noticed several good places in his travels—trees and hollow trunks and barn corners—and he goes there when he knows a storm is coming, and he sets inside, too, and keeps out of the wind. Birds know the wind, remember; they know it a lot better than we do because they use it and live in it every day. So they sense a change quickly and react to it. You and I just put on a coat and keep doing what we were doing; they start to get ready and find cover right away.

"Birds have a way of fluffing up their feathers, too, to help protect them against the cold, probably like putting on a fur coat because it keeps them warmer than if their feathers were down flat. Just the way horses and cows grow longer hair over themselves in the cold months. Dogs, too, even Beans. And Macawber. Then when spring comes they shed off the extra hair or fur and can stand the hot days, too."

Cully tromped noisily over the crusted land. That was about the length of any discussion we ever had. But I was never in doubt that he was thinking and figuring and learning and wondering every minute of the day, whether he spoke or not.

When we reached the Baileys', Cully and I went to the back, a screen door covered with a nailed-up sheet of oilcloth to limit the draft during the winter and, so, shutting with a muffled thump rather than the sharp bang such doors on taut springs had in summer. We knocked and went in through the dark, wood-smelling shed, knocked again, and then into the overly warm kitchen with a lamp on over the sink and one over the table, the wood-box full.

When the door opened, it pushed back a purple and red roll of cloth she had laid across the door sill to stop the draft. I nudged it back in place.

Margaret Bailey was there, sitting at her table, not much expression on her face at all, her hands kneading slowly on her apron in her lap. She just gestured with her head toward the next room, a small room that linked the kitchen with the parlor. In the winter, it also had a bed so that they could sleep down where the fire was and not have to go up to the cold bedroom above, which they had closed off by hanging a quilt over the doorway to the stairs. Leaning against the bed was their warming pan.

In that room on a straight-back chair against the wall sat Ben, his wool winter coat on and buttoned with small brown shreds of wood stuck to it, gloves still on, his body slightly slumped forward. Though not tall, he was a broad man, and his relaxed figure overflowed the chair. He had no pulse at all.

"Margaret, he's gone," I said back into the kitchen as gently as I could. She made no response, except a little nodding to show that she knew. A heavy man, his heavy clothes, hard work outdoors, and a final chore of bringing in armloads of wood had conspired to overburden his heart.

"Let's move him to the bed," I said to Cully. "OK? Think you can do it?" He had not stopped looking at Ben since we entered the room, and I thought he might not want to touch him. "Take his legs and I'll get around back and lift under his arms."

I wrapped my arms around Ben's inert form from behind, feeling the black and red wool lumberman's jacket and its big black buttons as I tried to get all the way around and join my hands. It meant putting my cheek against his upper back, and it was strange that that bothered me.

Cully did what he could to lift Ben's heavy legs under the knees, although it was more like guiding them. He was a stocky man, and his dead weight seemed much more than lifting such a person would have been if he had been alive. But we got him up onto the bed and laid him there on his back, fully clothed, jacket, heavy black shoes, gloves and all. Only his gray cap was off, lying on the floor by the chair where it must have fallen when he died and tilted forward.

"I'll call Dr. Handley," I said through the doorway to Margaret.

She nodded, still sitting.

I cranked up Central on their old telephone and got the message to Handley who said he would be over soon, seeing as Ben wasn't in a hurry and wasn't going anywhere. I was glad that Margaret had not heard how he said that. He meant it well because he was used to deaths and could handle them all with an impersonal manner which was necessary to his work.

But Margaret would not have seen that. Ben was a long-time husband, the only person she knew for many years, father of her two grown children and the three that had died. He had been out in the shed to get wood for the stove and had come back in, dropped it in the bin, gone in to take off his coat, sat down and died without saying anything.

And she had not said anything to him except the comment a person makes just after supper, maybe a remark about the weather or the stove not drawing well or what had to be done tomorrow. I think that was why she was so quiet now; whatever it was she might have wanted to say was too late now. And she knew that the hardest thing to bear would be that if she wanted to talk or make even a comment about the weather now, there would be no one to hear it any more. She had seen this in other homes, seen the loneliness and its withering effect on solitary women, and, when her mind was least expecting such a thing, it had happened.

I guess that was what prompted her to ask the two of us, "Can I get you any food?" It was a startling question.

"No thanks, Margaret," I said, embarrassed. It was not at all what I expected, and I added rather foolishly, "We were just finishing supper. We're real sorry, Margaret. Dr. Handley will be here shortly. You know how to reach us when you need something."

"All right, then," she said, almost drowsily. "All right. Thank you. All right. All right," as if talking to someone in her memory, someone not there in the house at all. Then she looked straight at Cully and said, "We'll miss him, won't we?"—said to a boy who had never before seen Ben.

"Yes, m'am," Cully said. "We'll miss him a lot."

And we went back home and tried to finish supper, but it was cold. "Maybe we shouldn't have moved him," was the only thing either of us said for a long time, and I said that, I'm not sure why. I guess I was just feeling very uneasy.

CHAPTER 12

Cully

It isn't so much the dying. It's the not knowing what to do.

When Pa died, I just walked and walked and didn't know what to do. I try to learn now and understand the new things that Doc shows me and teaches me, and I can do pretty well with most of them. He has liniments and I know which one to fetch when he asks me. He has bellows I can turn for a true heat in the forge. He has set me to tending the animals, and I can do that.

But I still don't know what I should've done when Pa died. I didn't say the right things, I didn't help, I just made Aunt Clara leave and made the house get left alone and empty.

When we went back, Doc and me, to get my things, it was like going to a different place even though I knew it and recognized it and could walk the floor from room to room in the dark. I didn't realize how little stuff we had until we went to get some of it and there wasn't much to get. I wonder if it still sets there, the piano and all, just drying out in the wind and the night, or if somebody has come in and settled down, finding an empty house and a piano to play.

Doc's telling about the hawks made me wonder about them, too. Because if they have to hunt all the time for food, what do they do when the food is gone in the winter? He says they see it even better, but what I mean is, how can they see what's not there any more? Mice and ground squirrels and rabbits and such don't stay out in winter, I don't think. And when that prairie wind blows in the storms with the cold so sharp it cracks the tree limbs, no little animal or even a hawk can stand that. Even a person can't stand it.

He has taught me lots of things about the land, sometimes strange things that make the land seem very uncomfortable and scary to walk across. Like the fact that it has hidden holes in it, holes where people tried to have wells for water but went away and left the holes, and now the holes have grown over and are hard to see when you're walking across a field or a yard. Doc says people have fallen in them and disappeared and not been found for years even, especially if they were alone at the time and just dropped through. Even if the old well-hole had a wooden cover on it, the wood's probably rotted, he says, and if even a boy steps on it he'll go right through. The idea of falling into a darkness is what bothers me, not knowing when you'll hit or what the bottom will be.

While we are eating supper, we get a call to go over to a neighbor's house. Someone says there's trouble and we go over to find out what, and help. It's hard pushing through the wind coming over the empty fields; I have to turn my side into it and squeeze my head down against my shoulder and, after so long, the muscles ache from the strain. Doc knows these fields, he says, so we don't have to worry about well-holes here. Way ahead we can see the little, wavering, yellow light, and we head towards it, the ground crunching under the hard soles of our shoes.

It's a kitchen light I see as we get close, even with my eyes watering in the cold and squinting away the unclearness. Doc seems to know the way, and he takes us in the back shed entry, a dark, wood-smelling room, knocking and calling twice with no answer, and into the kitchen.

An old woman sits there, quiet, not seeming to notice that we have come in. She is in a brown farm dress with white flowers on it, with a shawl spread over her shoulders and her apron on, and she's twisting the checkered apron in her hands even though she doesn't say anything.

I follow Doc into the next room, and at first I don't see the man. There's plain painted walls, an old iron bed painted gold, and several dim, framed pictures hung on the wall, one of a woman on a swing in front of the sun, with the tree showing just off to the edge of the picture. There's a small table with a white-and-blue basin and a white pitcher.

I look where Doc is standing, though, and I see the man sitting still in the chair, looking like a big, dark bear and he still has his winter coat and black working pants on. But his eyes are not looking at us at all. They don't seem to be focused, just open and sort of faded, not noticing anything.

Doc says something to the woman in the kitchen who just sits there, and I know from his tone that the man is dead. The man's face seems slumped down, not just because his chin has dropped down on his chest, but because the bristly skin has eased down and hangs low toward his jaw. His hands, with his gloves still on, are in his lap, sort of crossed between his legs, as if he just sat down to rest and couldn't decide what to do next. What I can't look at and can't not look at is his tongue. It sticks a little through his mouth and pokes out. I wish that Doc would push it back in and close the man's mouth.

Doc asks if I think we can lift him to the bed, and I think we can. But the man is awful heavy, and the strange soft weight of his legs slides out of my grip because my fingers are so short and because I don't want to hold him too hard. I try to cup my hands under his knees, just like cupping them so's water won't spill out, with the thumbs just beside the fingers instead of separate.

It's his softness that bothers me. It's like Pa's face when he went, with all the muscles still there, of course, but not holding the face just so, relaxing it into a face I had never seen before even though I knew who it was and knew what he should look like, but he didn't.

This man's legs, even through his heavy work pants, feel much weaker than they probably are, but they are very hard to hold, my hands too small and slipping off each time, and it takes Doc doing most of the work to get the man up onto the bed and straightened around so's he can lie down right. He sets the man's legs up on the quilt, black high-cuts on and all.

The room gets dim, and I can feel my head turn cold behind my eyes, and I know that I have to sit down now until I can focus my eyes again. The only place is the cane chair the man had been in, but I sit and let my head rest forward a bit, not fighting against the cold feeling, and just stay for a minute with my hands in my lap until it goes away. Doc doesn't notice. He goes into the kitchen and says something to the woman and rings up on the telephone and talks to someone.

Then I stand up. I do it slow in case the feeling comes back. But it doesn't, and I look at the man on the bed. There's no rising and falling of his chest and stomach. His hands are set beside him on the quilt, and, when I touch his gray cheek, he is already cooler than he was before. His tongue doesn't show any more.

I go into the kitchen and see that even though we have been inside for many minutes now and the kitchen is very warm, Doc and I have on our coats. The woman still sits there, and she seems to be rocking even though she's not in a rocking chair. Just swaying back and forth a little bit from her hips up, hands clutched in front of her, the twisted, faded red-and-white apron still wound into her lap. She asks if we would like some food, but Doc says no and explains that we have our own meal waiting for us back at the house.

I can see the woman don't know what to do. The man came in and died there, and she don't know what to do. All she can do is sway slow in her straight chair and say "All right. All right" in a little mousy voice that I can hardly hear.

I step toward her and want to tell her it *will* be all right, because I know that's the right thing to say, but she looks up straight at me suddenly and she says "We'll miss him, won't we, young man?" Then she looks away, at the stove I think.

I understand what she means, and without thinking at all I answer like I was her boy and say, "Yes, ma'm, we'll miss him a lot." Then I squeeze my lips together hard, and I touch the back of her pale hand, so thin that blue veins show and the bones can be felt right through, and she turns the hand over and its skin is rough and holds mine for a minute and gives it a very strong squeeze and then lets go, and she starts swaying back and forth again.

Going home, the wind is at our backs, and the walk seems shorter and not so cold.

Chapter 13

Doc

I made arrangements for Harold Brower and a couple of his men to go out to the Culbertson place and pick up the piano and some other furniture and store it in part of Henry's barn that he didn't use. I didn't tell Cully about this and I waited until he was at school that Wednesday to go back to the house and help Harold get the piano loaded. I am not sure why I did not tell him; it just made me uneasy to do and I wanted to have the furniture moved first and then tell him.

Of course, I knew the letters were there.

Brower's old chain-drive truck arrived about nine o'clock that morning, soon after I had pulled into the yard. We greeted each other and commented on the wind and then went in and I pointed out the things that should be moved out.

"Why're you interested in this?" he had asked.

"Well," I said, "that's a good question. I've got the boy for a while, it seems, and I suppose I feel a responsibility for whatever is of value in the house. I guess it's his now."

"Just leave it be," he advised.

"Yes, I know. That makes sense. But I'd hate to see even these few things get taken or just dry up or rot just because nobody took notice of them. It's all right: I'll leave a note, and I'll give the sheriff a list of what there is so he can see that it's all there. He knows we're not stealing it . . . not that anybody would care, most likely."

"I don't understand it," said Harold, "but like I told you, you're paying for it and I'll do it." It was a solid and workable philosophy: disapproving, not understanding, a bit nervous though sensing no actual danger and willing to do as told because of . . . experience, I guess. Trust, maybe. A deeper awareness that his worries were phantoms and not real.

The piano was awkward and heavy, its weight seeming to be mostly on one side, but the four of us struggled it onto the bed of the truck, its little rollers creaking under the strain of turning as we rolled it back. Then came three chairs from the kitchen, the table, a rocker, a lamp that, for obvious reasons, had not been plugged in, one picture from the wall, the old trunk, a few tools from the shed, the plow from the field, harness that lay on the dirt floor of the barn where Clara had left it. And that was it.

Harold and his men drove slowly back down the drive and turned toward town.

I went back into the house, a plundered dry-gray derelict building with sliver-producing boards, gaps in the shingles, ready now for whoever came along next to try to find a life on this land. The wind would work on it, the winter's crippling snows, the hard and deadly sun, and gradually the house would fade into the land.

Perhaps the loneliest sight in the house was the torn yellow-white shade on the window near Cully's bed. It turned the window light into a squalid golden, black-specked heat that reflected off the walls and exaggerated the trapped buzzing of a few doomed flies, their shadows moving under the shade with a sharp snap against it now and then. On the sill, the fallen ones on their backs, unmoving.

The plain-walled small parlor room was empty, looking even smaller now, nails protruding nakedly from the wall where someone had once hung two pictures; the kitchen had nothing but remnants of dishes and tinware, cupboard doors narrow and open. I had the strange compulsion to arrange everything neatly, to set dishes in stacks and be sure things that remained were in some semblance of order and balance. I set the tinware fork and knife side by side.

Back in what had been the small main bedroom, only a wooden chest remained, and that I had intentionally not given to Harold for removal. It was a kind of imitation cedar chest perhaps, and had a tarnished brass latch that caught and held the lid down. I had first seen it when Cully and I had been there, and this time I had opened its lid, then the inside compartment at one end, and again seen the letters inside. I wanted Cully to have them, but I felt protective, too, not wanting him to read them if they were bitter or about the end of his family. Some were in a woman's handwriting; some in harder, heavier writing on coarse paper. I resolved to intrude into their messages and decide whether or not Cully should read them, feeling already that the chances were very strong that he should.

I wanted to read them, too. Their postmark was Connecticut.

I stuffed the bundle into a paper sack I found and carried it furtively back to the car, tucking it down beside my seat so Cully would not see it if he happened to come out to the car when I got back.

CHAPTER 14

Cully

Sometimes I know that when you remember, the thing changes a little. I know that time changes, and my recollection of the thing isn't the same as when it really happened. And then tomorrow if I try to think back to my remembering, it will have changed again. I know that now.

Like when Pa died and I ran to him from the pump: I know that running was only for a few seconds really. But when I dream it, the running is so slow, and although I run as hard as I can, I don't seem to get much closer. I feel angry that I can't run faster, then I can see that not only am I running but I am watching me run, too. I am both the one running out to Pa in the field and at the same time standing still and just watching it all. I see that even the mule's stomping his leg for flies is slow, and the swishing of his strong and black-tufted tail is slow.

The dream never lets me run all the way to Pa; something wakes me up each time. But it is so clear that whenever I try to think back to that day, I remember it the way it is in the dream more than the way it truly was. At least I think so, so that now the dream is more real and the true recollection of that day is almost gone.

I think that that dream's affected other thoughts, too, and when Henry comes to get me again at school, it happens like the dream. We are working on our seed projects, each one getting four different seeds to grow in a box full of dirt so we can recognize the shoots and record the different rates of growth. Then we have reading time, and I have one of the encyclopedia books that tells about hawks. Mrs. Carty says I can read the best of any in the group. She told Doc so. I also like to learn about the states and draw maps, and I can spell Louisiana and Connecticut every time.

I walk outside at noon recess after we eat our lunches at our desks. It is a nice day and for no special reason I am one of the last to go out. Many days, weeks even, have gone by since Henry and Frankie stopped me in the road that I have just stopped thinking about it at all. So I do not expect anything.

I come out the door onto the covered porch area and kids are playing in the yard. When I reach the top step, before I start down, I see that about five or six of the boys have gathered over by the green water pump, and when I step down onto the first step, I hear someone say very low, "There he is."

"I'll get him," says a mean voice, and even in the chill of that second I know it is Henry who said it, and they all look at me without turning their bodies. But Henry turns.

I keep going down the steps, angling across as I go down, so that when I reach the bottom and stand on the big concrete slab there, I am closer to the pump and the group than I had been when I was at the top.

I remember that the air is clear, it is springtime, and that even though I am still twenty feet from them, I see them very clearly, sharply, and the air is crisp and bright. I can hear crows overhead, and out in front in the yard I hear the younger kids laughing and screeching as they play tag.

I stop at the edge of the concrete slab and look at the group of boys by the pump, not understanding what they are doing. Then Henry sort of tugs up on his belt with his thumbs, takes a deep breath, and starts running toward me. He has on his highcuts, so his steps are slow and sound heavy. The rest stay at the well. I can hear him breathe as he runs toward me, and it seems like he's running for a mile or more because he comes on so slowly. And I think, "What's he going to do? He's just running hard and what's he going to do?"

Nobody at the pump says anything. He's running not toward me but at me, I can tell that now, and I just stand facing him right on the edge of the concrete slab. But I realize that I am calm; I am not afraid. I am thinking, and I know that I am standing there and he's running at me, but I am watching the scene also.

I wait without moving, and I can see that that bothers him. But he does not slow down any. Then somewhere inside I know what I am going to do, and it comes without thinking but just from feeling, from knowing, and I wait.

His running seems like a big machine or a big animal more than a person, and I am surprised at how calm I am because I know he wants to hurt me. He is surprised, too, and I think that he has not got any other plan than to smash into me. He's like a huge rock that has broken loose and is tumbling down a steep slope: he can't stop now and yet he's surprised because he hadn't figured it out right and what's happening isn't what he thought would. He can't control it, either. He just keeps coming on.

I stand on the slab, about four inches off the hard dirt ground, and I let him come and come at me. By now I should have run, he thinks, but I haven't. I should have put up my fists, but I haven't. I just stand there. And then when he can almost touch me, I lean forward a little and put my leg up so it is straight out and brace myself. He can't stop and he runs his big stomach hard right into it. The air gushes out of him in a loud "Ooooofff!" and he sits down hard in the dirt right where he had taken his last step. I am like a tree. I don't move.

I am still standing there and I am amazed at what I have done, amazed that I did it so easy and without any fear. I just stand there and look at him sitting on the ground holding his stomach. Then he gets up by spinning slowly away from me on one knee but still holding his stomach. He pushes himself up with his other hand and walks bent over back to the silent boys standing at the pump who say something to him and then stare back at me. But they don't do anything.

I turn and go out into the school yard and find somebody to talk to because I am shaking now, nervous not from fright at all but just because I am starting to understand what happened, and it is so grand, like being chosen for a prize when you do not expect it so that you don't have time to be excited beforehand but only after. I talk a lot of nonsense . . . and I can't even remember now who I talk to . . . but I know that I have to talk just to keep touching what happened so that it does not just end like a dream and suddenly turn out not to have happened at all.

Later that night, as I think about it, I can relive it clearly. I can even hear the squeak of Henry's boots and his scout knife jangling against something on his belt as he runs at me. The black of his boots and his pants and his belt, his brown shirt, and the hard, dark scowl on his face are all clearer than ever I saw anyone before.

But what seems strange to me is that while I know it must have taken only a few seconds, it goes so slowly. When I raise my shoe up flat and he runs into it, I can practically count and say in my mind, "Wait . . . wait . . . not yet . . . not yet . . . NOW!" And the next feeling is his stomach hitting my foot and then gone as he sits down with the wind knocked out of him and his strength gone and his mind changed.

I do not know why Henry was running at me that day or why he wanted to bother me. He never told me, and he never did it again.

CHAPTER 15

Doc

The letters had been in a compartment in a low chest of the abandoned house, so that after a person lifted the chest's lid, there was a wooden side section across one end with another lid. In that were the packets of letters. They were wrapped in a dry, yellow, crisp paper, a small number in each packet, folded neatly, held with plain string. Some were dated or in postmarked envelopes, some not. The odd thing was that at the bottom there were five recent ones, all from within the last two years, all addressed to Cully, all unopened.

After Cully was asleep, I sat at the kitchen table and put the opened ones into a kind of order, first using the ones which were dated, then trying to fit in others that seemed on similar ideas or referred to the same time of year. Following the course of a conversation when you hear only half of it is difficult, but the packets generally had been saved in a sequence and the occasional references to the seasons proved to be a good assist in finding the flow. Occasionally one letter was far out of place, suggesting that someone had returned to it much later and reread its message. They had been saved by the person who received them, I thought, the woman, and they gave a full picture of about two years in the lives of a couple who, it was clear, decided to marry. The letters then stopped.

I read the packets through several times during the nights of the next weeks, easing into the private lives of people whom I did not know, discovering even something about my own emotions and memories as the courtship and engagement, the plans and hopes, and the underlying hint of difficulties were set down innocently in fountain pen and wide-lead pencil, the kind a carpenter or lumber dealer might have used.

With each reading, I saw the two of them better, and I felt that I was getting to know them so well that if I met them in town, I would speak to them as to old friends, even though they would never have heard of me. Yes, I would think to myself, I have read your letters.

Anna, the young woman who had received the letters, was seventeen when the first one was saved, for the third letter referred to her birthday. She had saved them all, even the first.

> *Dear Anna,*
>
> *I enjoyed meeting you at the social last Wednesday evening. My brother had to force me to go, but now I am glad that I went. The days since then have gone quick because when I came back to Willimantic I had to go right back to work.*
>
> *The fellas who work with me at the farm get a good laugh and say that I am a lot slower now because I am day dreaming all the time. I hope it doesn't embarrass you to know that I am thinking of you.*
>
> *Next month I plan to visit David on a weekend and I hope to have the chance to talk to you again.*
>
> *Your friend,*
> *John Culbertson.*

John Culbertson, who was to become Cully's father and whose life ended on a hot, dry field under a blazing southern Illinois sun, apparently received a warm response to his first, bold letter, for he proceeded to write to Anna nearly every week. Their meetings also continued, as John used visits to his family home in Ashton (as subsequent letters revealed) to see "My lovely Anna" as he later called her in his letters and, after more than a year, ask for her hand in marriage.

A year after they met, in a letter written from a distant place not identified, he wrote:

There are things here you would not believe. You must come here. Ashton seems such an old-fashioned town now. It seems asleep and unexciting. I want to get away. I want to move West and make my own way. Oh Anna, if you could just see this place!

In that ancient hope lay the seeds of what later became disaster. His wanting "to get away" had become a drive, a hunger not to be answered by logic or appeals to stability or her desire to "wait a little while" to please her father, who seemed not at all happy that such a young daughter would leave home for so far away.

But in the last several letters, the "I" had become "we," and Anna was inexorably bound into the fateful movement toward new land. For John, at least, it was to become a sad and literal trek that older pioneers had used as a metaphor for death itself: gone west.

But what of Anna, the lovely brunette dressed in white in the posed photograph kept by John and now by his son as a haunting reminder of the woman who had started west, had borne a son, and who had now vanished from the story?

I did not read the five unopened ones, the recent ones addressed to Cully. John had not seen fit to show them to his son for some reason. I wasn't sure what benefit they would be now, but I kept them tied with string with the other packet.

The image in the photograph seemed to haunt me, too, and the names of the little Connecticut towns echoed somewhere even though the exact recollections and places had long since faded, replaced by my Anderson years, lost in the dust of my own journeys across the land.

Of Anna, now, we had a wind-scuffed piano, a pack of letters, a silverplate-framed photograph, and a son. Yes, I had returned to the abandoned house with a borrowed truck and some helpers and had brought back the old piano. It had to happen. For me, at least, it had to happen. He probably would have been content to let it all stay quiet.

But he was a strong boy now, and at last I judged it was time.

When he had come up from the cold cellar with some potatoes for supper and we were getting the meal together, I tried to start. But just beginning under those circumstances was impossible. It wasn't just a friendly conversation, it was things I had to understand, and chatting about them while peeling potatoes was not going to work. So I waited.

Cully saw the face-down photograph and he tried to act as though he had not noticed the letters. He ate his meal with extra concentration, sometimes examining his fork as though it were a new object to him.

Then he asked again about the farrier's tools I had out in the barn, the horse knife and the buttress. He knew what they were. He knew a buttress cleaned hooves. He questioned me about the tool I had that I had used to repair a horse's worn teeth and the farrier's stand which held the hoof still while it was being worked on. He continued the busy, distracted series of questions, a very strange conversation, virtually a repeat of the one we had had before: he was doing what he could to avoid the eventual questions from me, and I was almost unable to ask what I wanted to. Yet when the conversation started, it flowed in a flood.

"Why don't you just throw away old horseshoes?" he asked, referring to the large box of them out in the barn, the earlier questions back again as a way of starting.

"You never throw away a used shoe," I told him in a voice that sounded odd and school-teacherly, like a preacher's or somebody reading poetry. "Used shoes have lots of uses, like holding the barway of a fence. They're likely to come in handy. So you keep them."

"People save things a lot," he said.

It was a startling statement, a clear shift to the items on the stand, a cold, hard leap from the iron familiarity of the horseshoes to the fragile tension of recollections near the surface yet chained into a deep past.

"Yes," I said, "they do," and waited.

He was silent. Clearly, if this conversation were to go further, he wanted me to begin it. I picked up the silver-rimmed photograph, looked at it, tilted it toward him. "Did you know your mother?"

"Yes," he said, still looking at his plate but seeing something far beyond, even as I saw a lovely woman posed in white in front of some photographer's trees.

"Did she die?"

"No. She went back," he said, and vaguely gestured out the window toward the horizon. It was a statement. There was no trace of bitterness. She had gone back . . . home, I assumed.

His way of saying that gave me at least a modicum of admiration for his father. Whatever else had happened, even with the withholding of the letters mailed from Anna to her son, John had otherwise kept Anna Culbertson's image clear and positive in Cully's mind. She was indeed still the "lovely Anna" in the white dress.

"It was a couple years ago," he added. "She had to go back."

Had to go back, he said. John had been a gentle man at least with memories. He had, after all, kept the letters his wife had saved. But what reason could have made her leave Cully? It was hard not to feel a bitterness toward her.

"Back where?" I asked, knowing part of the answer.

"East. To her home. To the Strongs, her family."

It was like lightning striking just outside the window, instant thunder so shaking and inescapably close that the fear and the delight merge in a moment of terrible ecstasy, dread, and danger. Yet all I said was the name: "Strong?"

"That's her family's name. It's my middle name," he answered. "John Strong Culbertson. It was her name before she married Pa. Anna Strong."

I *knew* the name "Strong," knew it somehow from a sense of loneliness and a hollow pain. Before I was Gunnar Anderson, before the orphan train and the shotgunned hawk, before the state veterinary college and my marriage, there had been another solitary boy who had a name like Strong as well. I did not tell Cully that, yet. It was important now to learn his tale, console his understanding, share his brief and monumental past.

"Was Aunt Clara always with you?"

"No," he said." She came from Ohio, too, a different part, when my uncle died. She said she was just staying a while, but she didn't leave. Pa didn't like her much."

"Was she your mother's sister?"

"No, my uncle's wife, Pa said, his brother who had gone to their town in Ohio and come down with fever."

"And she joined you and your mother and Pa on the farm?"

"No."

He did not continue at once, as if the heavy weight of this memory was rising through his chest and it would take some time now to let it ease out in pained, breath-taking steps.

"No. Ma was gone when Aunt Clara came. Pa needed somebody to help with the farm and with me, I guess."

Cully still stared toward the plate, saying what he knew would some day be asked, poised on the edge of crying and not looking up to make it be so.

"She said he had to look after her now that Jedediah was dead. Brothers had to do that, she said. They argued a lot at night. But she stayed . . ."

"And . . . ?"

". . . and she used the strap a lot."

It was a calm sentence, so quiet and frail. There were layers of subterranean tears beneath its soft expression.

"We left that there," he said.

I knew he meant the strap, and, remembering that I had tried to find her so that she might have the boy back, I knew now that Clara's departure was a blessing. For quite different reasons, neither wanted such a reunion, and for the first time I felt relieved that Clara had vanished, my own guilt at keeping Cully now turned to a released sense of rescue.

I, too, had known a strap. And when Mr. Anderson died, my only feeling was that same relief. On that night, as Mrs. Anderson and I sat in the darkened parlor, she straight and veiled and weeping, I in an old, small suit with the heavy casket on two saw horses in the middle of the room, I felt unburdened, lightened, lifted out of a suffering I could not explain, a suffering whose cause existed somewhere in the old man's soul and not in my behavior and, as such, was not escapable or understandable. But I was free of it forever.

The mention of the strap ended our conversation. It said more than needed to be spoken.

I went into my room and got the unopened letters. "Cully, these are for you. They were in the house."

He went into the sitting room and was very quiet. I could hear the envelopes opening, the sheets of paper being shifted. I hoped these would ease the stinging memory of the strap. I left him there to read and remember, and after a short time, perhaps fifteen minutes, went out back to the barn.

The next weeks passed as reenactments of routines. We went to Hardesty's farm several times to be sure the cows were doing all right. We drove far to the Lockridge farm to tend a skin rash some of the Herefords got from some bad feed he had picked up at a bargain price. We stopped by a few times to see if Margaret Bailey was all right, taking her some fresh-dressed beef that Hardesty gave us for payment.

Dr. Daniels' Veterinary Medicines served as much for humor as for healing, and their presence was, ironically, a tonic to my swirling mind: one read "Wonder Worker Lotion—the most wonderful healer ever known for sprains, sores, or wounds, either new or old harness galls, cuts, sore shoulders, scratches." It was, of course, the panacea reinvented every year and sold by traveling men in carts to all who would wash away the infirmities of hard work.

It truly was hard, sometimes, to answer with a straight face when a farmer with an aged, faltering horse would ask, "What have you got to help old Pete, Doc?" When the same liquid might be said to serve as eye wash, distemper cure, and hoof dressing, the farmer might as well have brewed his own liniment as paid some of his scant money for these impossible nostrums.

Cully went to school for his second year, helped me in the evenings and on weekends, read a great deal from books the librarian at the Perkins Free Lending Library in the school let him borrow, and never mentioned Aunt Clara again.

The photograph with the studio's name and address on the back, the familiar sound of the name "Strong," and an accidental phrase Cully had used—John Culbertson's brother "had gone to their town in Ohio" . . . "*their* town"—these hints conspired to give me restless, excited nights, already sensing that some time, not too long now, we both would head east, retracing the long-weathered wheel ruts of John Culbertson and his wife, the lovely, sad, absent Anna.

CHAPTER 16

Cully

I see the picture on the shelf and know that he is going to ask about it. That's okay, I say to myself, because he wants to know, but I feel different inside. I feel tight, like a cage that wants to hold something in. I think about telling him right out, but I don't do it. I ask about his blacksmith shop, his tools, his medicines. He answers them all again, but he knows.

At last he takes Ma's picture from the shelf and shows it to me again. He asks if I remember her and if she is dead.

I do remember her. I can hear her voice and feel the buttons on the edge of her sleeve when she hugs me. I can remember her baking day. I would sit up on the counter beside her mixing bowl and board and watch her roll the dough. I could just fit there, with cabinet doors behind me and on one side. It was a perfect place. The smell was sweet and dry, just like the yellow-white dough with white flower dusted on it that she flipped over and rolled back onto itself again. Then she'd cut off a little corner and push it to the side where I was sitting, as if it happened by accident. She'd say, "Oh, there's one for you," and I'd eat the soft, sweet dough in a way that made it last as long as possible. It didn't matter if it was doughnut dough or cookie dough or pie crust. I liked them all. That was before I started to help Pa a lot with the work and chores.

I look at her picture quickly. It is from before I was born. I never saw her look like that at all except when she sat down at the piano and played. She changed then. She would play and sing in a soft, clear voice that followed the piano sound perfect, and she'd sing about red sails in the sunset and one that began "Just a song at twilight when the lights are low." When she played, she looked more like the picture that set right on the piano in front of her than any other time. And she'd see me watching and she'd smile at me. Then I'd sit on a chair right beside her, but I couldn't play. I'd just sit and watch her hands touch the keys and make the song sound out.

We moved a lot, and I remember that the packing up again was always hard and made them angry. I don't remember how many places or what each one was like.

Sometimes I went to school but sometimes we were too far from a school and Ma tried to teach me to read and cipher by herself. She had a book she used, a regular big-people's story book, not a student's book like we had in class, and when we finished it, she would start in from the beginning again if she couldn't get another book to use. She said that I was a good student and could learn fast, and she said she would teach me to speak a language called French when I was older if I wanted to learn how. She showed me how to write and hold my hand with the pencil if we had some scraps of paper to use, but now and again she would seem to be just looking at her hand and then the other one with the ring on it. Then she'd remember that we were writing and we would start again. She sat close and smelled nice.

When we moved to the next house from Ohio, the work was hard. Pa said we did not get enough rain, and Ma asked why did we come here then. We never bought any new things any more, and we had to patch everything and mend our clothes and not wear shoes. There weren't any more books. The only thing I got new for a long time was my hat, and Pa got that later when he said I'd need it if I was to work with him in the fields.

They argued a long time some nights in their room.

When she started out that day, I had just spilled some Old Dutch Cleanser in the kitchen beside the sink and thought she had come over to scold me about the white powder mess. But she said she would be away for a while and I should help Pa all I could. She sounded different, and she started to have tears roll over her eye lids and down her cheeks. She dabbed them with her small white handkerchief that had the lacy edges, the one that had been my Christmas present from the half-dollar that Pa had given me. It made me scared. She stepped down the back step and went two or three steps away. Then she turned back and said, "Good-bye, Cully. You must stay here and help your Pa. Be good. I love you."

"Where are you going, Ma?" I asked, crying now too, knowing, but I didn't know why.

"To the train," she said. "Away . . . home."

"Isn't this home? Can't I go with you" And she just turned away and put her hand to her mouth.

She went out to where Pa had the wagon ready, and they drove down the dirt driveway with dust rising and were hidden behind the dust even though

I could still hear the wheels and the creaking and the horse's steps, and the sound continued, emerging from the dust like the train's whistle and churning from somewhere in the morning fog down in the river bottom near Wilson. Now and then the dark shape of the wagon showed, but the dust blotted it out again.

Hours had gone by when Pa came back from the depot, and he was alone. It was late in the day and we hadn't done much work that day. He didn't talk at all during supper but I knew what he was thinking about.

"It's all right, Pa," I said to him. "We can do it all right until Ma gets back," not asking him the questions that were in my mind. He nodded his head without saying anything except "I know," but he didn't smile like I thought he would. I cleared the table and poured the hot water into the basin. He was still sitting at the table as if studying the check pattern, but his eyes looked further than the pattern, not seeing it, not seeing anything. I scrubbed the dishes and set them to drain, but he hadn't moved. Then I dried them and put them on the shelf, put the spoons and knives and forks loose in the drawer, hung the wet dish towel over the string that was tied to two nails hammered in along the side of the sink bench.

Pa was still looking beyond the pattern. I did not know what to say and so I said nothing. I went into my part of the bedroom, pulled back the blanket, sat down and pulled off my shoes without untying them, and went to bed with my clothes on. Through the two doorways, past the piano, I could see him there at the table, and I turned my back and faced the wall so's I could close my eyes, even though it wasn't late and I wasn't tired.

CHAPTER 17

Doc

When the news came that Andrew Muriskow had passed on, it was as if someone had told us that a certain tree had gone down. Wasn't it down already? someone would ask. I don't remember seeing it the last time I passed the Corners.

Andrew was a man who had migrated from Massachusetts so long ago even he had forgotten when, and he lived here so long even he had forgotten how much. Skillful in logging and sawmills in the East, he had become a potato farmer here in the plains, maybe *the* potato farmer is better said, because there weren't too many men who would try that risky crop in this soil. But Andrew did, and he survived, and he became known as "the potato man" to people who never knew his real name and never asked. So when they said that Andrew had passed on, it did not seem to mean anything until they said, "The potato man died." Then we were all surprised, and then surprised again that we had not seen him in so long that we had thought that he had gone West already. Someone said that he had "left us," and right away the men in the store got to arguing about how can a man leave us who hasn't been with us for so long that nobody remembers him anyway.

It was a way of deferring the realization that life was limited and that we were older now.

I asked Cully to go with me to the funeral on that raw day in April so Andrew would have at least two people there to pay last respects. He had not had much livestock, but once or twice he had called me in to treat a sick horse and I had enjoyed his solitary and gruff company. He was not a talker, although what he did say showed a sardonic wit and was often entertaining, but never was he one to reveal a thing about his own background except the broadest facts. Had he been married? No one knew. Did he have family to be contacted? No one knew. Did he leave his farm to someone? Did he have a will? No one knew.

But I did know this. It was something Mrs. Anderson had told me many years earlier, and like a melody it had drifted into my knowing almost without my being aware. Now it came gently back. I could hear her voice and see her standing by the sink, her left hand still on the raised pump handle as she drew water to heat on the stove. She turned toward the coffin in the parlor and said, "No matter what, each of us is one and cannot be repeated." Then her hand brought the pump handle down and the water filled the kettle in a bold, splashing, bright stream.

So, on that wind-swirling, cold April morning, Cully and I drove out to the farm where the service would be held in the parlor. The sun that day was a vague and colorless presence which lighted the land without warming it, and small weeds and dirt blew across the ground and slapped against flapping pant legs. People in town ducked their heads into their shoulders as they walked.

South of town several miles was the farm, then a long drive leading to an isolated house perched like a barren sentry post among a few trees nearly in the middle of Andrew's land. Etched glass decorated the front door, and the front hall boards thumped with every footstep. We were shown into the parlor by the minister who had posted the hand-written notices of the service at the store and post office.

The parlor was dim but not empty. Three other people had come to Andrew's bleak and barren house on this cold day, and they sat in dark clothes with always at least one empty seat between, in a line of Andrew's heavy and musty parlor furniture and white, scarred kitchen chairs, the number of chairs astonishing for a person who lived alone.

The minister, Rev. Howard B. Mills, had come over from Dutton to officiate, and he stood in front of the center of the fireplace with the mantle behind him. Throughout the short service, the wind pushed down the chimney and burst against the black boards Andrew had nailed together and set into the fireplace to prevent a draft, blocking them at the bottom with two bricks and draping a black shawl over the top and down the sides. The boards leaned forward and drew back, their thumping an uneven and hollow drumbeating behind the minister's humdrum words.

He read from the Bible; after passing out thin hymnals, he led the five of us in a hymn that barely made a sound; and he read "The Service for the Dead" from the back of his hymnal, read in a monotone devoid of interest or caring, read with a preacher's voice so far from natural speech that it made the day colder.

Nowhere did he mention Andrew Muriskow. Nowhere. The service was anonymous, read and recited and done without one reference to the human being for whom the service was given. It was as if Andrew had been no one at all, and the absence of any calling of his name left me angry, empty, wanting to stand and chastise the minister for not at least trying to do something to make Andrew's passing a human event worthy of naming.

Instead, I just rose at my chair and stood silently until the minister noticed me. "Yes?" he asked.

"May I speak about Andrew?" I asked.

"Why yes, brother, of course you may. Please do," said in a voice so sickly sweet and smooth that I started to become angered again.

"I knew Andrew a little," I said to the small gathering. The minister was watching me with a smile of benevolence masking his inner heart, and one other person's head—besides Cully's—was up and looking at me. Two stared at the wall. "It seems right that someone should say something about him, for he was a person who made his home here, was a quiet person, and left this world without notice or preparation or family, as far as I know.

"When I came to his farm to look after his horse, he did not chat and tell me the latest news in his family. As far as I know, he had no family. We did speak, and I enjoyed his spare wit and the occasional wry smile he tried to keep hidden by turning a bit away from me.

"He never inquired into my life, either, yet I felt that he was a caring person and I know that he took good care of his stock and his farm. He worked hard, doing almost all the work alone and making enough to avoid loans and foreclosure and crop failure. He did not dress fancy and he did not spend much time in town.

"It might sound like an unusual and sad life to someone who did not know him. But Andrew always seemed to be at ease with himself and the world, even though it made him work hard for little return. Instead of seeing his life as different, he seems to me to be a lot like the rest of us. And I want to say that I enjoyed his acquaintance. He paid his bills, he was a smart and hard-working man, and such a person should not leave us without our taking notice." I paused trying to decide what to add, but after a long delay, said, "May he rest in peace" and I sat down again.

"Thank you, brother, for those most warm and graciously kind words about the deceased," and he went on for a few more sentences of closing ritual which I did not hear before we all stood up and went to the door.

The minister stood there and shook each person's hand as we left the house. I expected the hand to be cold or weak, but it was warm and solid when it shook mine.

Outside, the wind blew dust at us and we immediately turned away from it and backed and sided our way to the car. In the car, I sat for a minute or two and looked at the house with the dark-clothed minister leaving, locking, and hurrying, coat flapping, to his own old car.

The house was plain, two storey, one fireplace, with evidence of once having had a front porch because out ten or twelve feet from the front door, set into the grass and pebbly dirt, was another front stoop, a large, rectangular slab of gray granite someone had brought from far to be a monument to their settling down. Now the stone rested alone, several feet from the house it used to serve.

At the top of the roof in the front stood a stained copper weathercock, driving hard now into the harsh wind, its tail swerving back and forth in clear indication of the wind's force.

And I saw again the etched glass in the door. What had looked like decorative lines from up close was now a large tree with its boughs sweeping up toward a white-etched and crystalline sun.

We were the last to leave. "Let's go home, "I said to Cully.

"Yeah, let's."

Only then did I realize what he might be seeing, be remembering, and I felt a cold and hollow thoughtlessness for having brought him with me.

I felt a need to get him away from there, for it seemed to me now that all we saw was death and yet he should not know that any more than he already had. I wanted some way to change his life, change the mood of it, let him see life and warmth and kindness and . . . I did not know exactly what or how to say it. But the idea began to weigh on me and haunt me. I was now responsible for his life.

CHAPTER 18

Cully

Winters are very hard on people. We try to do the usual chores and help on the farms, but it is difficult to get around and we sometimes just can't go anywhere.

There is part of last winter especially that stays in my mind because of the deep snow and the wind and the fox. The storm seems to come from nowhere, just a gray darkening of the sky from the west, and the sign that it is going to be bad is that everyone begins to move faster and not smile at all and take things in and close barns up tight.

It starts when we are at the Radbourns' farm in their barn to help them with a cow that is sick, and Mr. Radbourn stands up and looks toward the open barn door very serious, and then walks outside. He stands in the light rectangle of the door as if he is in a dark picture frame, and he looks up at the sky, turning his head so he can see the horizon all around. The wind lifts his hat, and he slaps the back of his neck and catches it from blowing away. Then he comes back in the barn to where Doc is and says, "It's going to be a bad one." He is frowning and sounds tense.

I think he is talking about the cow's sickness, but when Doc says, "She's going to be all right, I think" I know that it's something else that he means. He goes over and hits his pipe against the wall and sets it on the shelf by the rows of dark green Half and Half tobacco cans. He looks out the manure window.

"It's fifteen, now," he calls, checking his outdoors thermometer on the side of the barn.

Doc says, "Come on, Cully, we have to get home" and I can feel that he is worried because of the tone in his voice.

As we drive, I see behind us the gray-white sky which rises up from the ground to higher than clouds usually are, and it fills the sky and dims it into a different duller light than usual. As we drive past houses, now and then a person is moving fast, some running, and they are carrying things inside or rushing animals into their barns, and the sight makes me feel cold.

Doc is not saying anything, but he isn't just driving either. I can tell he is thinking because I have seen him be this quiet before and his look tells me that he is concerned. The wind hits the side of the car and bumps it with sudden small shakes.

"When we get home," he says, "herd the two cows into the same pen and put lots of hay there for them, enough for several days. We'll have to do most of this in the dark because I'm going to close the big doors and draw the canvas over the doorway to block the wind, and we'll nail the split grain bags over the windows. Macawber goes in, too, and leave him lots of food."

When we get there, he drives the car right into the barn and we jump out and start working. "Come on," he says, "we've got to move quickly." I get the cows in from the pen outside, and Doc takes down the poles that hold the barn doors open and swings them shut. He has trouble because the wind has begun to blow, and he has to push the second one pretty hard against the wind to close it, and while he does that, the first one swings open again. So I help him by holding the first one shut, and then he pushes the second, then swings around it and pulls it shut so's we are inside when it closes.

The wind is heavy, but the way to tell how strong it really is is to hear it, and it seems to slam against the barn doors and shove them back. Then he puts the cross-bar in place to hold the doors shut. Even so, it rattles some with the wind as he draws the canvas across it and hooks it on the nails. Already we can see our breath in the dim barn air.

Macawber doesn't mind coming in, and he's already found some food and starts to eat. The cows are glad to be in with lots of hay and feed. Then Doc and I go out the side door and swing the big iron latch arm down tight to hold it closed. Beans goes inside the house with us.

The sky now is over us, towering way up and so thick and gray you can't see back into town at all, and cold stinging specks of snow have started to fly through the air.

We each hurry to take in many arm-loads of wood, and they fill the woodbox and spill off onto the floor in another pile just about as big as the woodbox itself. There is so much wood we can have a good fire for weeks.

Then Doc shouts, "No, Cully! Not like that!" so sharp that it startles me. "Not near the fireplace or stove!" He is almost yelling and his face is stiff and different, like somebody else's face. He has never spoken to me like this before. He wants me to make the stack neat and to set the wood further away from the stove and hearth. I do it, even though it means that some of the wood is out into the room rather than along the wall. Later he says he didn't mean to speak like that.

For some reason the house seems hard, the walls not warm and nice like they usually are, but cold and stiff and more like part of the outside than the inside. Doc checks the food shelves and sees that we have some boxes of things and food in tin cans. We have an electric pump in the well house, but Doc knows that we may lose that and not get water from the faucet, so he checks the old small, green hand pump that sits at the end of the sink, and it works fine and water spurts out of it. He catches some in a pot and sets it aside. He smiles at me, "I knew we shouldn't get rid of that," he says, patting the pump.

When Mr. Lucas put in the electric pump, he wanted to take out the old one on the sink, but Doc said he'd better leave it, just in case. Mr. Lucas said, "You won't be needing that any more" and muttered to himself. Doc said later that that was just his disappointment because Mr. Lucas is so excited about having more people receive electricity and he thinks it is a miracle and everybody should give up the old ways.

The storm hits us soon and although it comes hard, it grows even stronger and sometimes shakes the house, with the wind whistling as it tears around the corners and flaps the shutters against the sides of the house. "That's one thing we forgot," says Doc, as a shutter bangs the outside wall. He hurries through rooms and goes around to the sides away from the wind and opens the windows enough to pull the shutters closed and latches them with the inside latch, but the ones on the storm side he can't get from inside because he doesn't want to open those windows and have snow and wind roar in. So he pulls on his coat and hat and goes out, and I hear the shutters bang shut in a hurry and then the click of the latch sometimes, and Doc is back coming in the door with snow all over his coat and he tightens up his fists and arms and lets out a breath that tells me "My Lord, that is cold!" We can hear the wind in the chimney making a whistling moan.

It seems like a long time that we have to stay inside, but he says it is only a little more than a day. During the evening, before we go to bed, he reads a long poem called "Snowbound" out loud, and it seems as if it could have been written right here. I get sleepy and miss some of it.

During the night, Beans gnaws on her bone just as if it's summer time, and I pull the scratchy red wool blanket up to my nose and I am still cold. That's when I invite Beans to sleep on the bed, even though Doc doesn't like her to do that. She steps onto the bed as if she knows just how to do it, and she curls around a few times and then settles down. She is heavy and presses the blankets down and I can't move my feet, but I can curve up against her and feel warmer.

When the wind dies, the clouds have moved off, the snowing has stopped, and the sun gleams with such a glare on the snow that it is hard to see. It is late morning and the sun is high, but it does not give us any warmth. The milk has frozen and pushed the cap right up the top like a column of white ice, and he says, "Try it." So I chew on the milk ice and it crunches and crackles in my mouth and is delicious. Then we let it thaw into a pan.

Doc gets the wood stove going and we put some slices of bread on the long forks and toast it over the heat, turning it just a beautiful brown. He's mixed some sugar and cinnamon, too, so we put that on the toast and have a special winter-storm breakfast before starting to see what we can do outside.

The kitchen door swings in and we can open it and see that the snow is half-way up the screen door. But that one swings out, so there is no way we can push it against all that snow. The side door swings in, too, and that does not have a screen door, but we have to open it very carefully or snow that's packed up against it will tumble into the room.

Doc has remembered to keep a shovel inside for us both, so he opens the side door, stands inside the house, and begins to make a path out the side door through the snow. He has to throw the shovels of snow up very high to get them off to the side.

What we find is that not far outside there's a low spot, a place where the wind swept the snow away into a great swirling curve, a drift Doc calls it, and we can walk almost on the ground with no trouble so he uses it as part of his path. Beans likes to go into that area, but the deep snow stops her.

Doc says that one time the snow was so deep at the Andersons' that they had to go out an upstairs window and were in danger of dropping down into it way over their heads. I don't know if that is true or just one of his smiling stories.

It takes us most of the day to shovel a path to the barn. Doc says that it doesn't snow the way it used to. He says when he was a boy, the snow would be way up by his head and shoulders, but now it's barely up to his waist. Then he looks at me with no smile, waiting to see if I will figure it out. Then he laughs when I do.

We often have to stop shoveling and go inside to get warm. Doc says it must be below zero, but it seems to me that cold just reaches a certain level and after that it doesn't matter much what the numbers are, it is cold. The fire in the stove keeps the whole room warm, and sometimes it hurts at first to come in from the air that crisps my nose to the warmth of the kitchen.

In the barn, the cows seem fine, their breath coming out in clouds, but Doc throws a blanket over each one's back because even their extra hair won't help much today, and Macawber moves around so much that he seems not to notice that it is so cold. He's very glad to see Beans again, and they nuzzle each other.

Beans then starts acting strange. She faces off into a corner of the barn with her head very still and her tail wagging, and she makes a little whining sound in her throat. Then she walks back and forth in an arc, always looking into the corner with the tail and throat working. She looks happy, excited. "Something's over there," says Doc, and we go slowly over to see what it is, our feet swishing in the hay on the floor.

It is a small red fox, and it is so scared or cold it can hardly move. It makes a feeble little sign of being dangerous, with its lip pulled back and a kind of hiss coming out, but it isn't going to attack and we aren't going to hurt it.

"Odd to see a fox here," says Doc. "Must have been searching for some eggs or something to eat. Now he's stuck with us for a few days, I guess, and we'll have to figure out what to feed him. Don't get too close to him yet," he says, "he doesn't know you. He will, after a while." Then he tells Beans to "Come on. Leave him alone," and after we check the feed and hay for the cows and clean up behind them by tossing their steaming manure out the window onto the pile outside under the snow, we go back inside and my hands ache as they start to get warm again.

Later I carry out a tin pan of scraps for the little fox to eat, and I give him some water in a tin dish, too, only he'll have to drink that right away or it will be frozen. I wanted to take warm water out so that it would not freeze so fast, but Doc tells me that warm water freezes quicker than regular water. I don't see how that can be, but I take regular water.

I sit down several yards away and watch him, and soon his black nose twitches and tells him that there's food there and he forgets about me and moves over to it to eat. He tears his food and growls a little as he eats, looking around once in a while to be sure there's no danger. I don't move.

Only when I get back in the house I realize that I did not notice the cold this time while I was sitting with the fox. Doc asks, "How is he?" and I tell him "OK."

The next time I go out to the barn it is late afternoon and I can't find the fox anywhere. The pan of food is empty, the water has ice on top which I break, and I set more food scraps in the pan. I call to him which I know is silly but I do it anyway to let him know that I am his friend, but he doesn't come out.

Macawber wants to get at the food, but I have brought some for him, too, and I find a wooden crate and break open one end, and I set that over the fox's food hoping he'll go in and get it. I should have brought Beans with me. She'd help me find the fox.

The cows can't go out, and we milk them there, the warm milk making suds in the pail, and then turn them loose to walk around in the barn. The car takes up some of their walking room, but there's no way to change that now. The fox won't bother them, though they might get huffy if they see him.

Outside, it is a white world now. Other drifts have blown the snow up high against one side of the barn, and the opposite side has hardly any. The snow seems bluish and as the sun sets it shows some red and green sparkling, too, and then it makes shadows where it is piled up.

Night comes early in the winter, and I know that even with the storm stopped, the snow will be around us for a long time, it is so deep. So Doc banks the fire and we go to bed early and sleep very long in the chilling darkness. We wake up in the cold room again, with only a few embers left in the stove, but Doc gets the fire going again right away. Beans jumps down before he sees her.

That morning, we talk about shoveling a path to the road but it is so far we decide just to make a trail out to it by walking and stomping the snow down. What happens is that we stomp it all right, but that packs it under us, and soon we are walking on solid snow about three feet off the ground. It lets me see very far and be part way up the trees as we pass them.

Some people are passing along the road on foot, and Mr. Coburn had one of the old rollers that his big and powerful Percherons could push, so he has rolled the snow down and packed it, and people can walk and drive their wagons on top. There aren't any cars out, though. I guess everybody's car is in their barn and snowed in for a while.

The snow lasts almost a month before it all melts, but the fox is gone long before that. He never does get comfortable with me coming into the barn, so he always hides somewhere and eats after I leave or sit down far away.

But one time while I am in with the door open, he must have run out. After that his food is not touched and we do not see him again. I did see glimpses of him from time to time before he leaves, and he looked strong and healthy. But I know that wild things do not like to become pets and I never think that I can keep him. Beans runs around in the barn sniffing for him, but he's not there.

When we get back over to Mr. Radbourn's farm, I tell him about the fox, but he just says, "Fed him? You fed him? I'd-a shot that damn critter right between the eyes." He seems very sure that that's what he would've done. It's hard to like Mr. Radbourn after that.

CHAPTER 19

Doc

Out in front of Walker's store, tucked back against the store in the shade most of the day, is a plank bench. The two one-inch thick boards are shiny; even their iron-hard knots gleam from pants seats and callused hands rubbing and rubbing over the years.

Daily during the warm months, two old men come to sit on these planks. They arrive separately in the morning sometime between nine and ten o'clock, each coming in talking and explaining why he is arriving when he is. Each knows the ritual, does not interrupt, and finds his same spot, day after day after day. Then they sit quietly, sometimes for hours, and watch whatever is in front of them, usually the few people who come to the store, sometimes a passing car or wagon, occasionally a truck. They mark the details, keep a mental record of the recurring events as if they are unique and not the same as yesterday and the day before that and the ones long back into the darkened months.

One of these old men is Evan Benderson who once owned the store and, like any general store proprietor, is known to everyone in town, so everybody who arrives greets him and asks "How ya doing?" "How's this weather suit you, Evan?" "What do ya say, Evan?" while moving past and into the store. It is the great question that never is supposed to be answered.

Evan came to this area with his grandfather who had some land given to him by a relative who had gained it from another relative after the Civil War, and Evan began selling necessaries like seed and tools and blankets, gradually increasing the stock of what he sold until he finally had enough items to call his place a general store. His wife died seven years ago during a harsh winter. She had gone out to the coop to gather the eggs, and it was several hours later before Evan realized that she had never come back inside. He sold the store, and within weeks began sitting on the bench. He was the longest occupant of that place.

The second person was Eliphalet Armitage who had been in the Spanish American War, been wounded, mustered out, and come out west to try farming. Eli had never married. One day five years ago, he left his poor farm in the morning, came to town, and sat down. He left before sundown when someone offered him a ride, and that became his pattern to this day.

Eliphalet and Evan seldom had a conversation beyond the opening one of explanation. One would grunt and gesture with his head in a certain direction, the other would look at whatever it was and say a coarse "uh-huh," and they would simply sit and watch. If what they saw was surprising or novel, you'd hear them say "Huh!" in a surprised kind of way. If what they saw was humorous, the "Huh!" had a hard, deep-voiced smile to it. Most of the time, the response was a soft puff blown through the nose. These few sounds told their stories, their thoughts, their opinions.

People did not find them amusing or worrisome or plaintive.

They just saw them as an expected part of the front of the store.

That was why it was shocking to see only one of them there one day late in the morning. At first it was hard to tell what was wrong. The looker had an uneasy feeling, like seeing a wall where for years a picture had hung but today was not there anymore and nobody had told you about removing it. Or when a man one morning has shaved off his mustache without saying he was going to do it. There is just that odd sensation that something is different, but at first you can't tell exactly what it is. Then you say, to nobody in particular, didn't there used to be a picture on that wall? Knowing that there had been and wondering how many days had gone by before you noticed that it was not there any more.

"Am I right in thinking someone is missing?" people wondered.

They were right. Someone was. There was only one old man on the store-front bench.

That was the day that my haunting thought became clear. I decided that I would start back east to find Cully's mother and my own family, if I could. I did not want to become an empty space on a bench with people not really remembering whether or not I had been there yesterday.

Chapter 20

Cully

Sometimes there are times I would like not to remember. Yet whenever I think of them, I know every detail and relive it as if it is happening again. This is one of them.

When I walked to school, Beans would go with me about half way. There was a little rise in the road near a telephone pole, and I would tell her to sit and she would, without a noise, and she watched me go on to school. I know because I looked back many times, even just before she was out of sight, and she was still there looking at me. At some time she must have decided to go back home, because she wasn't there when I walked back in the afternoon. She'd be at the house, and she would come out to meet me with big jumps and her tail wagging.

Doc said that her hearing was starting to go bad, maybe because when she was abandoned before Doc got her she hadn't had much food for some days and now it has weakened her hearing. As far as we knew, it might have weakened her smelling and her eyesight, too. Her loss of the sense of smell was hard to tell, but the eyesight was surer because sometimes if I walked toward her from a distance and a direction she didn't expect, she'd look at me uncertain until I got closer. Then she'd come fast with tail swinging back and forth, almost trying to make up for lost ground or as if trying to pretend that she just wanted to be sure.

The day I remember I am walking to school and she is with me, just past the old brown house that Mr. Malkowski lives in, just past the end of his yard where he has tried to grow some tall yellow sunflowers.

I am just walking, maybe pretending something to myself. I don't remember that part, and an old, heavy dark car comes along on the dirt road behind us and I move to the edge of the road but Beans doesn't and the car just keeps going right over her and down the road without seeming to notice. I know whose car it is. It's old Mr. Koniarski's car and he's driving and has on a blue workshirt and a work hat and his glasses and a gray beard and he stares straight ahead and keeps going as if he never knew that he had just run over my dog.

I run home to get Doc and we go back to the place and Beans is still lying there. She doesn't look hurt, but she doesn't move. I can see that her sides are still, but there's no blood and no broken bones showing. I can't remember what the day was like, but it was just in that part of the road where I saw a cedar waxwing once and it did not fly away from me when I walked up toward it and I knew it was not scared and I always liked cedar waxwings a lot after that. That's where Beans is lying and she stays there when Doc looks at her and feels for a pulse.

"Who'd you say it was?" he asks me again.

"Old man Koniarski and he just went over her and didn't stop." Now I remember that there was a breeze, because the wind fluffed the hair on Beans's neck and waved it a little, and I am happy and call out, "She moved. She's still alive. She just moved."

Doc says no, that she is dead, that it was just the wind.

Doc digs a grave for Beans out in the back yard near the corner of the shed, and we wrap her in an old sheet and set her into the hole carefully. We set her in as if she is sleeping, the way she used to lie on her side with her front paws bent. When she really did that, she would sometimes dream, and she'd make little noises like tiny barks down in her throat and when she made the noises her cheeks would puff out and her feet would twitch as if she was chasing a dream rabbit. That is how we lay her in the grave.

We need to find something she loved, Doc says, so she can have it with her, and I go back into the house and find the cow bone she used to gnaw on in the middle of the night and keep me awake sometimes. Doc says she will like that. Doc says it is right to bury something that was loved with the loved one. But I did not do that with Pa. I wish I had.

Doc and me fill in some dirt and pat it down gently around her, and then do some more. Then the grave is full and we mound it smooth and Doc puts a horseshoe up for a head stone until we can get a real stone, a flat piece that will stand up when it is sunk into the ground a couple of inches. And he says, "She was good dog and she brought us lots of companionship and good times. I think she enjoyed her life, and her end came very fast and without pain. We can be thankful that we knew her and that she found us."

It is many days, weeks even, before I can get used to her not being there. I would sometimes think I'd see her but it is just a shadow or a dark place around a corner. Every time I come back from school I think she will run out to me.

Then one day I guess I understand that she isn't there any more because when I come home from school I go around back and start to work on a piece of cow hide I am tanning and do not even think about her. I set the leather onto a frame and turn it again because I want to make a design on it and have it in my room. And then I see her blanket in the barn and realize I am not thinking of her.

"What's wrong?" says Doc when he sees my tears.

I do not answer and keep working with my hands and turn away from him a little so he won't notice.

"Thinking of your pa?"

Then I really feel bad because I wasn't thinking of Pa and do not think of him very much at all and I know I should. All I can do is nod a little with my back turned to him and my head down.

"Beans?"

"Yes," I say in a big burst of tears and he says something kind to me that I can't really hear. But I know that he means it's all right to be sorry that Beans is gone.

I know that everybody loses their dog or their parent sometime, but that doesn't help. I want to be a big person and just keep going, but I don't. Doc says he understands that it reaches into me and makes me feel as if I am the only one and nobody knows. He says he has felt it, too. I guess people do know and they don't. They have felt their sadness but it isn't mine. Just the way I can't feel theirs when they have a loss. That's what Doc means when he says it is all right. It is my sadness and nobody else can feel it, and if I don't, it will never be felt as it ought to be. So it's okay to go ahead. It's not wrong, it's just being a person.

CHAPTER 21

Doc

Beans' death left us with an empty house. For a while we left her torn, brown blanket in the corner where she slept, but then I took it out back, shook it out, folded it, and draped it over a stall railing in the barn. Even that was sentimental, although I was just trying to get reminders put away so that Cully would straighten up again. I did not realize how much that dog had meant to him until I saw the effect the death had.

His Pa's death had been absorbed and accepted and set aside. Not Beans'.

Putting Beans' blanket in the barn had been done with at least a bit of an inner thought that she would have liked to have her blanket in the barn because she liked to go in there and lie down on a hot afternoon, and she'd come back out when Cully came home from school and there'd be straw hanging onto her sides and underside, and she'd shake and the pieces would go flying off, ending with whatever was on her tail being whipped up into the air and left behind.

Her water dish went outside for the hens, and her food dish got washed and put into the cupboard on the top shelf with the big bowls.

My work went on at a decent pace: animals always needed some help somewhere. So did people. And traveling around a bit was a pleasant way to spend the spring days, to see the fields developing into many shades of green and the calves and colts finding their legs better each day and moving along close to their mothers.

In town one morning, Lem Briskman called me back into the post office section. "I've got a letter here for Cully," he said, "but I figure if it is anything, I should give it to you to let the boy see".

"For Cully? All right. I'll take a look at it."

He opened the brown wooden door that separated the store from the post office, reached around the corner into one of the small rectangles of sorted mail, and pulled his hand back with a white envelope in it. "Here."

"Thanks, Lem. He will be real glad to get some mail of his own."

The envelope was the usual size with the picture that said the Willimantic Star Thread Co. in the upper left, and it was addressed to "John Culbertson and His Son John S. Culbertson, Weed, Illinois." Added in the bottom left corner was a note: "Please find and Deliver." There was no return address, but across the 3¢ George Washington stamp was the circular black postmark: "Willimantic Conn. March 8." It was now May 3rd. The envelope was thick: it was either a long letter or a letter and a document.

Cully took the letter into his room and sat on his bed to read it. He must have read it several times, judging by the length of time it took for him to come back into the kitchen again. I stood looking out the window, waiting. To the west, the sun made wide shafts of light which beamed up across the sky over the darkening earth, rising away over us. The slow setting of the sun and the huge high spread clouds made the sky seem permanent for a few minutes. It reminded me of the times on the Anderson farm when I would lie on my back in a field and look at the clouds blowing through the blue sky, watching them steadily, hypnotically, trying to stare beyond them. Soon the clouds appeared to be still and I was the one moving rapidly as if on a moving bed, flying through space beneath white cumulus clouds.

I even gained the sense of motion, as if when I moved I would be in danger of falling off my earth-bed, even though I was lying in a wide and rolling pasture. It was an unforgettable experience, feeling the earth's rotation so dramatically, a steady and almost hypnotic rushing along underneath the sky, even with a sense of gradual tipping, as if some time later I might be spilled forward as my earth-surface rotated downward toward the vertical.

At last Cully came out of his room back into the kitchen.

I did not say anything, waiting for him to be able to begin to tell me his thoughts without my prodding or leading him. He was taller now than when I had first seen him on the hot, dusty highway more than a year earlier, and his face had lengthened with his growth. When he was thinking, his head still tilted as it had that day, and his knee-scuffed jeans seemed much like the ones he had had on then, although the belt he had now fitted him better than that one had. His hands hung at his sides, and in one was the letter.

"She doesn't know that Pa died," he said. "She thinks we are still on that farm or maybe have moved on to another one. She says she is sorry that she had to go, but that now her father is very sick, dying, I guess, and she has to stay there."

He paused, and I knew he was holding back the main thought he felt, waiting until his heart and his breath and the thickness in his throat relaxed together and would let him say it.

The western sky was purple now, darkening more rapidly, trees no longer offering any shadow and themselves fading and blending into the huge shadow of the earth on itself.

He still stood in the doorway between the kitchen and the parlor, backlighted by the setting sun's remnants over the table, head tilted toward his left shoulder. The lighting made me think of a painting by Rembrandt, with dark clothes and darker walls emphasizing his light skin. I turned to him, now mistily there in the fading light.

PART IV

The Letter

Chapter 22

Cully

The day Doc hands me the new letter from my mother is a hot afternoon, I remember, because at school our class had a special day outside under a tree to use the shade to be cooler. It is fun to go out, but it isn't school. We like being out there and the thing that makes it different is the sounds of the air, sounds that I don't hear when we are inside.

Doc tells me I have a letter when I get home and hands it to me in the kitchen where he had laid it on the table. He stands there waiting for me to open it and read it, but I take it into my room and sit on the bed and just look at it for a long time. I know that nobody knows me, only one person, and believe that if I open the letter my excitement will end and the words will be there.

I slide a finger under the cool, sealed, sharp flap and move it through, loosening it, tearing it in some places. Inside I can see the folded edges of white, lined paper like we use in school sometimes when the yellow paper runs out. They are folded neat and lift smooth out of the envelope.

I turn to look out toward Doc, but he is not there anymore. I listen but do not hear him. I unfold the letter and see that I have it upside down, so I turn it around and smooth the pages out on the bed with my hand.

> *Dear John and Cully,*
>
> *It has been a long time since I came back east, and I wanted to tell you that I am fine and think of you many times each day. I hope that you are well and that Cully has grown into a big boy who can help on the farm and make it work.*

I am writing to tell you that my father is very sick and probably will not live to see the summer. The hard times have left him without spirit, and I think he never has recovered from the disappearance of my youngest brother so many years ago. His eyes look soulless, and he seldom has spoken for months. It has been a late-starting spring here, and the frozen paths still are hard to walk on, so we have not taken him out at all. And now I think he is getting too weak to move.

Dr. Donnerts stops by at least once a week on his rounds, and he leaves Father some pills to make his pain less, but you remember how he is and he often will not take them. Mother keeps herself busy with her housework and small tasks, but I know she is using up time and, like me, is waiting for the end.

Then, we shall see.

I tell you this, John, because I know you and Father liked each other a lot until just before we decided to leave, and I want to let Cully know that his grandfather, who asked me about him and who wishes he could have known him, probably will soon be gone.

I stay busy by helping at the school giving piano lessons and by helping Mrs. Safriniak take care of her smallest children. That is the family that lived down the Hill Road past the schoolhouse, and it is easy for me to go there from the school. I have asked for a job at the thread mill and they seem to be encouraging, but nothing has happened yet. I was in Willimantic waiting in their office for my interview, and I asked if I could write while I was waiting, so they gave me this paper and envelope to use then.

When I left the farm I did think that after a time I might come back if things went better for you. But I know now that that will not happen. I need to tell you that Mr. Caldword the magistrate in Tolland has granted me a divorce and I now use my maiden name. It is how the people here knew me and I want them to know me that way again. I doubt that I shall ever remarry.

I really don't know what else to tell you. I am peaceful here but I miss you both and hope that Cully is a good, strong boy and listens to his father. I pray that you understand.

With best wishes,
Anna / Mother

It is very hard to read the letter because it is from someone I know and at the same time don't know, and although I hear a woman's voice when I read the words, I don't know if it really sounds like her voice or not. I sit there on the bed for a while and try to remember her voice, but it never gets clear. It may not be hers but just my imagination.

When I go back into the kitchen, Doc is there watching the sunset. I tell him what the letter says, but he doesn't ask to read it. He just waits and thinks and pretends to be looking out the window at something. The room is getting darker but he doesn't light the lamp and neither do I.

I pull a chair out from the kitchen table and sit down, and I put the letter on the table in front of me and press its folds down neat and flat on the yellowed wood. Doc turns around and then comes over to the other side of the table, and he pulls a chair out and sits, too. I can see that he is looking at me and I think he is smiling, not at something funny but just a pleasant smile that does not mind being seen or not being seen in the darkening room. I think he knows how I feel confused, and I think he knows what I am thinking.

In a few minutes more the kitchen is dark, and the white moonlight that lets us know where the tree and barn are does not do more than make a dull mist of light in the room. I almost forget that he is sitting there with me he is so quiet. Even his breathing is silent. The table is almost gone, too, just a hard outline shape in front of me. I hear him breathe a deep breath. Then his voice, not loud, says from across the table, "I think we should go find your mother."

CHAPTER 23

Doc

There are things that happen beyond all intention and planning, things so powerful that they seem to control themselves and not be chance or luck or fate. If it were in a book, the reader would scoff at it and say that this is too made up. But sometimes they do happen and we don't know why.

I did not know what was in the letter beyond the little that Cully told me, and I did not ask to read it, ever. Yet even carrying it had had an effect on me that startled me and made my senses seem to be dulled to everything except that one letter in my hand.

A memory of the piano came back to me, the piano and the picture on it, the piano and Anna Strong Culbertson sitting and playing for her son, her hands still delicate even after years on the land, her hair dark and glistening in the shaded tall lamp that stood beside her, her face emerging from the picture to be soft and real as her lips moved silently with the words of the song, as her eyes glanced again and again to the boy standing just beside her watching her fingers touch the keys and bring forth music.

Impossible.

It was a memory of a scene I had never witnessed. My preparation in science had put an emphasis on facts and knowing and experience, yet in this moment all that training was discarded for the first time in nearly two decades. Memory and fantasy and imagination blended to say to my senses what it would take my mind much longer to confess. Somehow, from Cully, from the piano, the picture, the letters, I felt that I knew Anna.

This awareness frightened me because I knew I could not trust my judgment about Cully to be honest and objective any more. And it frightened me even more because I had not felt a fondness for any woman since Marcia died sixteen years before, and in dying carried our son with her beyond the reach of any human skill.

It is a testament to human doggedness that a person can have a wife and almost a child one day and then be alone the next and still go on. It is anger and deep hurt and sorrow and helplessness. It is emptiness, a splintering at the very center we had carefully and trustingly built. It is as much an abandonment as finding oneself left alone in a desert without sustenance. Total loss of everything one loved; total loss of the self, even beyond the self.

A person then constructs a fortress and in it he places that part of himself that had been wounded and which would surely shatter if exposed to further pain. It is a place where others cannot come. Yet years afterward a thought casually, accidentally sprung out of nowhere can bring all those emotions back so fast that the event pulses again and pains again as if just done.

And he also can place a dark and granite vault around his heart, insuring that such a loss can never again occur. Life may be without a woman's love thereafter, but it is also without the inevitable pain. It is calmed. It is outward. It is observation and reaction and dedication to easing others' hurts. It denies memory. And it is, finally, alone.

Now, through objects, imagined music, and handwritten words to someone else by someone else, the vault had cracked and the frightening vulnerability emerged again, revealed so fully that it could not be suppressed ever, a blend of fear and need, of hope and dread filling the room of one's soul.

Now before me, his small hands still upon her letter, was the boy whose flight from death itself had brought human warmth back into my life.

My voice seemed blocked deep in my throat, stifled by the very swelling that made the next step in our lives as inevitable as the passing of the seasons over the land.

"Cully," I was able to say at last, "I think we need to go find your mother."

CHAPTER 24

Doc

The dark room swelled with an intense silence after I said that we should find Cully's mother. There had been thousands of clear, black nights with the crescent moon and myriad stars, with no sound of night birds or moving cars, no human voices sounding over the flat and cooling earth. But this was like the inner core of a deep cave, as if we both were even trying to keep our breathing from being heard. Only after a few minutes did I hear the slow and rhythmic ticking of the pendulum clock on the parlor wall, a sound like tiny hammer strokes making the space between seconds definite and separate and long.

It was not a silence of fear, but of emotion, of tension forming in the heart and being held there, a soft silence, a warm quiet shared by two people in separate thoughts and separate ways but still the same.

I moved my hand on the wooden table, a sound more minute than a mouse's walking across the floor. It was enough. When he lifted his head I could tell because his eyes drew in some of the fragile moonlight and revealed his face. I rose, walked around the table, and turned on the standing lamp just inside the door to the parlor. We now existed again fully, the next-room's light letting us breathe and speak again.

"I wish she could come here," Cully said.

I wanted to say, "So do I," almost did say it, but no amount of private and selfish yearning now should divide his simple feeling for his mother, and I had no desire or courage to reveal that I, too, had a vague and cloud-like dream involving the same woman. It is thus we think with our hearts and speak with our minds.

"I don't think she will do that," I said. "She had some reasons for leaving and . . ."

"Should I write back to her?" he asked.

"Yes, you should. She will need to know what has happened." Then, after a pause, "And she will need to know that you are coming to find her."

Again he did not speak for some time, and the parlor clock paced the seconds clearly into the quiet room.

"How will I go?" he asked.

"I will take you."

"You have to stay here. They need you here. Who'll tend to Hardesty's? Who'll help Mrs. Bailey? What will happen to the house and the animals?"

"I will work that out," I said, plans already forming within a great hope in my mind." But first you need to write to her and tell her that your pa died and that you are all right. Can you do that?"

"Yes," he said, as if he had not just assumed one of the most difficult burdens ever assigned to a child. I wanted him to write the letter, partly so that she would hear from him, not about him, and partly because his own innocence would prevent the letter from being too detailed and too sentimental.

I would not have known how to tell her all that had occurred in the last year and a half. My attempt at cold objectivity would have sent crushing news and happy news like an iron telegram. Cully's letter would be from her child's hand and heart, and my thoughts would not be in it to add a stranger's invisible voice to any words that she would read.

"Yes," I said back to him. "Think about it first, then write it. When it is done, we will take it to the post office and have it sent special mail. Wait a minute, do we know where to send it?"

"She doesn't say in the letter," he said. "There is an address on the envelope, but that's not her."

"We know the state. Does she say the town?"

He went back near the light and looked through the letter again. At least twice he went through the pages. "No," he said, "she doesn't say. But she does tell about a man there" and he shifted to another page of the letter, "Mr. Caldword who is a mag . . . i . . . strate, magistrate . . . what's that ? . . ."

"A judge."

". . . in some place called Tolland, she says, and maybe we can send it to him and he could give it to her because he knows where she is."

The unusual length of his sentence told me how excited he was. "All right, we'll try that. I think it will work."

He sat that night under the parlor lamp, working at the cherry desk with an intensity and focus he often brought to tasks. He wrote with his head tilted and his tongue slightly out of his mouth and moving, it, too, engaged in finding the right words to tell his mother that his father, her husband, had one day died suddenly on the hot prairie earth and that her son was now coming home.

CHAPTER 25

Doc

That was when we went to see Mr. Lockridge and I spoke with him about a loan on the land and house. His reputation was strong as a smart and good-hearted man who had helped people before, and as I had taken care of his cattle when he had Herefords and had helped his sick horse through a difficult illness, he and I knew each other fairly well.

In fact, it was with his help that I tried the idea of using electricity to help cure the weak leg of one of his prized pacers, and he was quite grateful about that. We had gotten some special wire and wrapped it, then placed it in connected rows between two thin layers of a wool pad I had cut for the purpose. At the end of the wire I put a controlling dial so we could increase or decrease the flow of the current to stimulate the muscles in the part of the horse the pad was on. After a few tries we got it right and the treatment speeded up the pacer's recovery and he was back to racing in a few weeks instead of several months.

That word spread, of course, and there were other horse owners, pacers as well as trotters, who sought out the treatment. So we patented the pad and Mr. Lockridge set up a small shop in which a man made more of them, and we sold them to veterinarians across the Midwest. He invested the profits which we shared, and now, two years later, I had some money built up which, with the loan on my land, I could use for this trip east.

It was difficult to judge how much we would need for I could not guess how long the trip would be, especially with its unknown result awaiting us. I just knew that I wanted it to go well, and I knew that Mr. Lockridge would support us to the end, whatever that might be, as long as I was careful with the money.

I contacted the state agricultural college and they put me in touch with a young man with a little experience who could take up my practice while I was gone. He turned out to be a fine person, eager and knowledgeable, and for two weeks he lived with us and came with me to meet the people whose animals I cared for. He had worked at the college itself, but he wanted to try being on his own, and this was a good chance for him to find out what that was like. His name was Jeremy Danielson and by the time we left, he seemed to have understood much about what needed to be done, and the farmers he visited liked him.

I mapped out the route and showed Cully what the plan was. Heading east was not something I had ever expected to do, for my life and work had become well settled in the broad area I covered and there had been no reason to consider leaving. Now, so suddenly that it frightened me, I had taken a loan on my place, gotten a person to take over my practice while I was gone, and planned a trip that a few weeks earlier I would not have considered, not knowing exactly where I was going or why or when I would come back.

The most bothersome part of it all was the uncertainty. It wasn't like a vacation trip, although I had never taken one of those either, where you know the plan from day to day and know exactly where you will stay and when you will return to the same life you had before. This was moving into a new world with no certainties, no guarantees of success. We might not even find Anna Culbertson. We might just have to decide at some point that we had failed and start back again for the Midwest, and even the thought of that left me with an emptiness I did not like.

And if we did find Anna, what would be the result? Would she want Cully back? It was a question that seemed unthinkable, and yet I had to remember that she had left him with John, a kind of abandonment of a child so unusual that it would have been easy to dislike her simply for that alone. But she had written to him.

And if she took him back, was I to turn around and head home? I thought about her so often that she seemed very real to me. It was difficult to remember that she had no idea at all who I was, that I even existed, and that all my mental visions of her had been one sided, not balanced by any thoughts in her mind of the man who had cared for her son for nearly two years.

So I planned the route filled with questions but sure that I wanted Cully to be with his mother again. We would head a bit north and join the National Road for our journey, leaving it only to visit a place where Cully had once lived in Ohio, the town named for the earlier settlers who had pushed west into the Western Reserve and taken the government at its word: land nearly for free if you will build a road. The early Strongs had done it and had created Strongsville. There I hoped to find some answers before we went the second half of the way.

Because it would not delay us more than a day or two, it was a workable idea and Cully and I agreed to do it. It was to be an odd journey into the known, the imagined, and the totally unknown, a significant change from the steady and predictable routines of my years in Weed, a change filled with both excitement and hesitation as a past was about to be set aside while an even older past would be searched for and, we hoped, discovered.

Our next discussion concerned what to take with us. Clothes, of course, so Cully would need some new ones. First aid kit. A spare tire and two or three inner tubes, a jack, a patching kit. A thermos jug for water. Maybe a small can of gasoline in case we ran out in some rural spot. Blankets and a pillow for the back seat, so Cully could nap some of the time if he wanted to. Our maps. Extra radiator hose and clamps. Rags for wiping the windshield. A tin to put cookies or other snacks in. A pair of mud boots. Our jackets, just in case we stayed into winter. That meant winter boots and gloves, just in case.

It is not easy to plan for a long trip when one is not even used to taking short ones. And this one seemed so open-ended as to be filled with a vague and mysterious quality of discovery, a sense of reading a book about one's own life and, in turning the page, not knowing what would be on the other side.

CHAPTER 26

Cully

We go into Wilson, and Doc visits for a while with a man named Mr. Lockridge. Mr. Lockridge is an old man who has some money because he has a cook and a man to drive him around and somebody who cleans his big house. I have seen them. We have been to this house before.

In Wilson, there is a store named Lockridge's, and there is a meeting building named Lockridge Hall, and one of the white churches, the one with the black shutters and the metal plaque on the front between the two doors, is named Lockridge Memorial Church. Once Mr. Lockridge met us at his farm and drove us out into the pasture in his big car. It was shiny and had a driver named George, but it smelled of cigarette smoke. Doc's car smelled like dusty leather, the way a car seat gets hot in the sun and hurts to sit on, and it smells like a car then.

Mr. Lockridge's house is up some gray, stone steps, because the ground for the house is up on a bank and the road in front is lower. The steps are cut through the bank so you step on the first step at road level but below the house level, and climb up between the cool carved sides of the earth held back by stone walls, and when you are at the top, you see the road behind you down below through the straight rectangle made in the bank for the steps. On each side of the concrete path he has a big evergreen tree, and Doc says they were brought here from Minnesota and planted just for Mr. Lockridge. He puts Christmas lights on them in December, and people drive by and walk by to see the lights on his trees.

The house is white clapboards with a green roof, but it is not at all like other houses. The edges are trimmed in maroon all the way around, and the shutters are all maroon, too. At the top of the steps you can see that it is a house with two storeys straight ahead but only one which spreads out to the right side, that part shaded by maple trees on each side. All around it is a nice lawn and some flower beds against the house. A man takes care of those.

A person in a dark suit lets us into a hall with a silver-edged mirror on the wall and a dark carpet running down the middle of the hall but for about three inches on each side. The hall goes deep into the house, it seems, but we are turned through the first door to the right, a high, heavy, shiny, reddish wooden door that opens without any noise at all. Mr. Lockridge is sitting by the window and has seen us come up the steps. He shakes my hand with his finger tips but never asks me any questions, tells me to take some candy from a box on a big, dark, thick table that is in the room on one side against a fireplace that looks as though it never gets used.

While Doc and Mr. Lockridge talk, I am allowed to wander through the house. Things are made of dark wood everywhere, and each hallway, like the long one from the front door, seems almost a tunnel into another world. In one room there is a bed and dresser and wash stand, and on the dresser is a marble top with silver brushes and ivory-handled combs as if a lady used the room as a bedroom.

The room I like the best is the side parlor, a much bigger room than the one in which Doc and Mr. Lockridge sit and talk. This room has two curved sofas in it, pushed back against each wall between the windows and facing each other, about twenty feet apart, and many chairs with soft, decorated padding with raised designs on the seats and backs. It even has some towering arm chairs, most of them dark green or black, and a few fancy little wooden tables near the chairs.

On the left near the door into the hallway is a grand piano, its lid always flat down until somebody wants to play says Mr. Lockridge because I asked him. But more important than that is that on the piano lid is a brown hand-held stereoscope like the one I saw in the store in Weed once. I love to put down the pointed hand-grip, look into the hooded eye pieces, and put a card into the rack along the track. It makes the two pictures blend together and adds depth to it so that it looks real.

One picture—he has a lot—is of some loggers who have just cut down a giant tree, and they are standing beside it and on it and posing. I try to move my head from side to side in order to see further into the picture, because in the back amidst the standing trees there are some other men with cross-cut saws, and they are not looking at the camera. On a tree in the back there is a large bird, an owl maybe, that has not been frightened away by their noise.

It is not hard to hear their voices and the sawing sounds, but I cannot see what they are looking at and it looks like something interesting. Another card has the entrance to Mr. Lockridge's store, with six well dressed people: two women and one man are going up the steps into the building; two men and one woman are walking through the door and down the steps to leave. The picture catches them in mid-step and stops them there in awkward positions.

I look again at the first card, at the men standing proud on the tree, and it looks like the picture I saw once in a geography book at school of a hunter who had shot an elephant. The dead elephant is on his side and the man with the gun is standing on the elephant while another man holds onto one of the long, curved white tusks and another stands on the elephant's head and holds out the huge ear. The elephant's eye looks as if it's open, as if he's just waiting for the man to step off him and he'll get up and go on eating grasses and leaves.

You'd think dead things would look different, but they don't. At least not unless you look close, like Pa's whiskers.

I hear Doc call and go back out of the big room into the hallway, and he's standing at the front door with it open and the bright daylight behind him. He looks like a dark statue.

I wave to Mr. Lockridge as I pass his door. He's sitting in his chair by the window and is putting a small blue booklet away on top of a gray-green ledger. He waves back.

The drive back is clear and warm and quiet, and when we get back to Weed, it is late afternoon. We pull in in front of Walker's store but we can see that the door is closed and there's an envelope stuck in the window edge. Doc reads it: Gone. Emergency at the Hanks house.

"Let's go see if we can help," says Doc, and he backs the car around and drives west, then turns down a dirt road that runs north across the fields. Each time we see a clump of trees growing, I know it's a house, and at last Doc says, "That's the Hanks place" and turns into the yard.

There are lots of trucks and wagons there with many people gathered out in the distance across a field that is just overgrown, no crop planted. They stand almost in a circle, and when we get there a man in bib overalls tells us that Betty Hanks' little brother, not two years old, has fallen into an abandoned well and is stuck down there "about ten, eleven feet."

"Went right through the boards, he did, and somehow he was directly over a well hole that ain't seven, eight inches wide. Just slipped in," the man said, sucking on an unlit pipe. "Lucky his sister saw him go or they wouldn't have no idea where he was," he said. "Can't hear him crying nor nothin'."

There are three shovels lying around, and the top of the well hole is scooped out to maybe four feet, and in the center of the scoop is the well. Men have tossed the broken boards off into the field and they kneel in the scoop at the edge of the small hole and peer down into it, sometimes calling his name,

Tommy, sometimes saying that it's okay and everything's going to be all right. But their faces say that isn't true.

There's rope on the ground, too, and a long pole where they have tried to reach to him or hook the rope onto him somehow, but they can't, and now they look around for new ideas, then look back into the hole, then around all over the field again. They don't know what to do. Shoveling didn't work, the rope didn't work, the pole didn't work.

"How long's he been in there?" Doc asks a man.

"Must be five hour, maybe more," the man says, never taking his eyes off the hole as if he expects the boy to slide back up and out just as easy as he went in.

Mrs. Hanks is standing off to the west about ten yards, staring at the place where her young son disappeared into the earth. Nobody moves. There's hardly any talk.

I remember what Doc said about other uses for horseshoes, and I try to think of something that might help get Tommy out of the well. Something that isn't used for lifting things up out of narrow places.

"Doc," I say. "What about the gripper things back at the store that Mr. Walker uses to get boxes down off the high shelf? They're skinny and they clamp shut at the end."

"That's worth a try," Doc says, and he tells Mr. Walker and he gives his keys to somebody who runs fast to a car and drives away in clouds of the dusty land. Someone else goes to tell Mrs. Hanks that they're trying something else, and she puts her hands to her mouth and has tears on her cheeks.

It seems to take a long time for the person to get back with the car and the clamp-pole, and then about five or six men go to get it and they all say, "Here, let me . . ." until a voice from the far side of the circle says, "Let Walker. He knows best how to use that thing."

No one knows that it is still a bright sunny afternoon or that the ground smells of spring sweetness.

Mr. Walker stands in the scooped-out part and straddles the hole, his heavy brown shoes working their way into a good grip on the earth. He lowers the clamp-pole until it gets in a ways, then he lets it go very slowly down farther until he can feel it touch something. "I think that's him," he says. "Hard to tell when you can't see."

He moves the pole around a little, turning it back and forth. His look is concentrated, not focused on the hole or the earth, as if he is seeing past them and into the soil. Then he closes his eyes and turns the pole until it seems to stop. Very carefully he squeezes the grip that closes the jaws of the clamp and starts to lift the pole back up, but he stops. "Nothing," he says.

He does this again and again, each time slowly and carefully lowering the pole after resetting his feet, one time calling out that he thinks he hooked the boy's shirt but he couldn't hold it. "Can't see anything. Hard to tell what you got," he says.

"Too much time is passing," Doc says in a whisper close to me.

"How long's it been now?" I ask.

"Maybe another two hours since we got here," he says.

Half the orange sun still shows above the wind-break trees to the west, and their shadows are lengthening across the field. Each person has a long shadow now, too, and there are different people. Some of the early ones have left to tend to their chores; others came as they heard the news. A few have gone to gather lanterns so the work can continue into the night.

"There," says Mr. Walker suddenly. And he starts to lift the pole back up, its straight pull difficult.

"What is it?" asks a man.

"I think I've set the clamps on his neck. Feels like his neck." says Walker. "A couple of you help me lift." Three men rush over to the scooped area and reach for the pole. "Get low and work your way to standing," calls someone, "then shift back down to the bottom again."

"Careful, now."

They lift slowly and can tell that something with weight is being pulled up the hole. "How're you know that you ain't choking him?" asks a voice. Mrs. Hanks sobs very loud when she hears that, and some rough voices tell the one who spoke to hush up. "I was just askin," the voice says.

"Hush up anyway," comes the answer.

The man near us in bib overalls leans toward Doc and me and says in almost a whisper, "Don't make no mind, does it, if he's got the side of the neck or the front if the choice is not to get him out at all? Huh." He spits a squirt of tobacco juice into the dirt.

Doc nods his agreement "I see his arm!" the man now at the bottom of the pole says, "Keep him coming!" They pull upward, like pulling a cleaning swab through the barrel of my .22, and then a small, limp hand shows at the top of the hole and then above the top, white and dirty in the gray evening, and a man kneels down and grabs it and tells the men above him to keep the clamp in place but to lighten the pressure. "Slow and steady now, boys," he says. "Slow and steady."

Then the arm flops over and the boy's head shows just at the top of the hole, then it's above the hole, and the clamp is opened and removed and two men reach in and inch Tommy out of the well hole. Now his shoulders are out, and they can get a good grip under his arms, so they smoothly lift him all the way out and lay him on his back on the dry stubble at the edge of the scooped earth.

Doc is there now, listening at Tommy's mouth, massaging his chest and ribs with both hands in a rhythmic pushing way I saw him use on a calf once. And Mrs. Hanks is there now, too, kneeling in the dirt beside Tommy and wiping the soil from his face. Someone lights two of the lanterns and sets them on each side of Doc and Mrs. Hanks, the kerosene aroma lifting into the darkening air, the light throwing shadows across the faces of the people, most kneeling or crouching now, in the silent circle of watchers.

I sit on the ground behind Doc and clean the dirt off Tommy's bare feet. They are very cold.

"Good, Cully. Now wrap his legs in your jacket and snuggle up to them as much as you can. We've got to help him get warm again."

He works well into the dark, massaging Tommy's chest, pushing breath out and into him, listening at his mouth for a sign.

Suddenly Mrs. Hanks walks forward and stands beside Doc. She puts one hand on his shoulder. "Let me take him," she says. "I'll hold him close and he'll know. Even if he is gone, he'll know. Let me take him." The men in the quiet circle slowly straighten up, and they start to turn and move away.

Doc, still kneeling, straightens back and she reaches in and lifts her dead son to her breast and rocks him there between the two lanterns.

When we get back to the house, I say to Doc, "You knew he was dead, didn't you?"

"Yes."

"Why'd you keep tryin' then?"

"I guess it's just natural to try anyway, to not be ready to admit that he's gone."

"Not everybody did that," I say. "Some just came to see."

"I know. But they understood, even if they weren't able to do anything. They understood."

"Understood what?" I think back to Pa's dying and my not knowing what to do. Maybe if Doc had been there we could have done something.

He stands at the sink, his hands on either side of his hips holding the sink edge, looking straight out the window. Then his head turns. "It's just natural," he says. "All creatures try to help."

He waits again, as if thinking something over. "Come here," he says, and I go stand beside him. "When I was about your age, I was out walking with my dog along a lane at the edge of the Andersons' field, and first one crow and then two and three started cawing at us from the overhead branches along the path. As we went on, they got louder and made a strange harsh croaking noise

I had never heard before. The dog and I went on and they got louder and more frantic and began to fly down and try to frighten us.

"Then I saw that ahead of us in the path was another crow, and although he seemed alert and able to walk, it was clear that he couldn't fly. We walked closer and the other crows . . . six or seven by now . . . were desperate and very loud. They came down to the branches just above our heads and they scolded and were as angry as I have ever seen crows get. They were trying to save their friend, I think, and were very upset with us for getting so near.

"The crow on the path walked fast to the side but he got into a place where some bushes met a fence and he got trapped, so with the other crows swooping and cawing right above me, I got down and put my coat over him and picked him up. Now they were really hollering and they flew at us and around us screaming all the way back to the Anderson barn.

"So I kept him and fed him until he was able to fly again, and I named him Jack. He stayed near the barn most of the summer, and then next year he came back again. But then he didn't, and I never saw him again. I think he flew off with a flock and had a very good crow life," he says, and he smiles at me.

It surprises me that I can feel my shoulders relax and my heart slow down. I didn't know that I had been worrying.

PART V

The Journey

CHAPTER 27

Doc

We left one clear morning and headed northerly toward Vandalia to join the National Road, following it through Effingham and into Indiana. Over the last few days, I had gradually made my good-byes to the people at the store, Margaret Bailey, Hardesty (who was none too pleased), and the rest. Jeremy Danielson saw us off, and because our way led us away from town, we did not see anyone else that morning as we left. It was well that we did not. The pull backward on me was nearly as strong as the pull forward.

Of course I got advice and criticism from the in-town people, with some adding a sense of guilt for leaving folks in the hands of "an untried man, a beginner," as they called Jeremy. Generally, though, I was more of a curiosity. I had not told anyone about my own background, so it was easy just to say that we were going to take Cully to his mother.

"Jest put 'im on a train for the Christ's sake," was Harvey Wilton's wisdom. "Don't you go, too." He was incredulous that I would travel that far just for a boy who was not even a relative. "What's he to you that you drive a thousand miles over bad roads just to take him home?"

I laughed at his disbelief and joked that I just wanted a little vacation drive, and the roads were not that bad any more; but inside me there surely was that gnawing question asked a thousand times in the night and never answered with a sure reason.

The brown dirt roads were dry now at least, and the wheel ruts which had lined them deeply during the spring had now dried, crumbled, and been worn down to small ridges that were no bother.

The first day took longer than I had thought it would, for we stopped in Vandalia at Craycroft Motor Company to get the radiator hose and they found another one that was worn and needed replacing. I had to pick up a pair of boots I had taken to Lockart's Shoe Repair, so I did that while the new hose was put on, and Cully and I took a few minutes at the ice cream counter at the Hotel Evans to kill the time, too.

So we started out, intending to stay along the way in places where people had cabins to rent for the night. The frequent availability of such stopping places was one reason—this and the better quality of the improved concrete surface—for traveling the National Road.

We talked about it on the way, a kind of history and geography lesson for Cully that I could learn, too, and that we could see first hand as we traveled. It was exciting to head into Vandalia and know that not many years before, a young Abe Lincoln had walked this street as a member of the state legislature going to the capital.

From there we headed east, retracing the direction if not the route that I and so many others had taken since the land was first opened for settlement. East through Indiana, Ohio, Pennsylvania, Maryland on the National Road, shifting in Cumberland to the Cumberland Pike to Baltimore, then north again into Pennsylvania, New Jersey, New York, and, finally, Connecticut.

The road was named and also numbered, 40, with black and white route markers replacing the old red, white, and blue bands that had been attached to telephone poles. I had no sure idea how long the trip would take, but I knew that there were many filling stations along the way and we hoped to drive more than a hundred miles in a day when we could. I had heard that a man once rode his bicycle from Zanesville to Cumberland in about four days, but that was back in the late 1800's on the road surface made of small packed stones that Jack McAdam had devised. This surface we were on had been repaired and was smoother now, so we expected to move well.

I was very aware of the ghosts we were passing as we went: old forts from the frontier days; places named for people who had settled there, won or lost battles there, died there. And the ghosts moved as well, moved past us in Conestoga wagons heading west or moved with us as drovers moved cattle or sheep or as farmers carted their crops in heavy freight wagons to sell in the East. These musings filled the air with voices, singing, calls, whip cracks, creaking wagons grinding forward under heavy loads, snorting animals; the smell of oxen and horses, the stench of spring mud and filthy boots, of cooking fires, sweat, heat, and dampness.

It was impossible to be alone on the National Road, no matter how personal and isolated one's reason for journeying. We were not the first orphans looking for family and future, but I may have been one of the few who traveled the road eastward looking for the past.

Near Terre Haute, we pulled into a Richfield filling station and the boy came out and pumped our tank full. He chattered the whole time, too, as if we were the first people he had seen for months, and Cully just watched him, never before knowing anyone as windy as this boy.

In pulling out of that station I swung the corner too sharply and the right front of the car rose over the rounded side of a white-painted stone, then dropped with the running board still a propped up by the stone intended to be a decorative marker. This was a new one, a need to jack up the car on the side and somehow slide it sideways off the stone. Men from the station came to help, several with ready advice and a sense of the mission's inevitable failure if their words were not listened to. Lifting, pushing, grunting, and swearing were the sounds of the afternoon until everyone at once seemed to give up and stop, and we still sat hung up on the stone. They set timbers under the car to raise its side and hoisted, but no one could quite move the stone. They declared it a mystery and sat down on oil cans and boxes and running boards to wipe the sweat from their faces.

The windy boy dashed to his bicycle and pumped hard as he sped down a side road near the filling station, dust rising from behind his rushing wheels. He had, it turned out, hit upon the right idea. What men could not accomplish, a near-by farmer's draft horses could, and soon a blue-shirted man in a slouch straw hat drove his team of huge horses down the road toward our stranded automobile.

"This your car?" he asked.

"Yes," I said. "We're stuck on that rock and can't move it."

"I know," he said.

"Can you do it?"

"I can't, no," he said, "but my animals can. You been trying to move the automobile. We're going to move the stone." He spoke to the horses and they dutifully stepped their large, hairy hoofs around to the side of the huge stone, stopped, and on command backed toward the car.

"Better get out again, "I said to Cully, whose fascination with these behemoth animals so dominated his concentration that he did not hear me until I touched his arm and said it to him again. "Better get out and let them work."

The farmer tossed his hat aside and got down flat on the ground to worm his way under the car in the gravel, dragging with him the stout chains he had had brought from the station. Some clinking and sounds of strain came from under the car. Then he slid himself back out, stood, walked to the front of the horses, and spoke to them again. Four men from the station again levered the car up about an inch off the stone, straining and tensing in a great show of strength and human power well beyond the energy they were actually using, speaking in gasping bursts of words to show how difficult their task was. You'd have thought they were lifting a granite mountain.

The farmer spoke softly again. Slowly the horses moved forward, stopping instantly at his spoken command which sounded like "hut!" Then they moved again, the chain gradually tensing, scraping along the running board, actually lifting that side of the car and then dragging the whole rock sideways and out from under the car. The men set the car down again with a great and unanimous exhalation of strength released. Of course I treated them each to a Moxie, and they clearly appreciated having had the diversion on a slow and unpromising afternoon. The farmer would take nothing, although he did bask in the recitations of exploits the windy boy told of his horses' other achievements. It was a delay but an enjoyable one, with only minor damage to the car, no bent wheel, no flat tire, and enough good yarns and interesting people to have made it an adventure.

One house we stopped at for a meal and to sleep between Richmond, Indiana, and Springfield, Ohio, was run by Josiah Brinkley who claimed that we were right in the midst of history, that Presidents and generals and even Jenny Lind, the Swedish Nightingale, had stayed in that house. Mr. Brinkley had a wonderful knack for enlarging on the facts, entertaining us with a long story which ended with a person named Basil Hall right there in his parlor writing that this was a place to "water the horses and brandy the gentlemen." Then he laughed with his face and hands and stomach, adding to the entertainment.

I could see from Cully's beaming face that he enjoyed Mr. Brinkley and his tales, and it was evenings like that which made the days less tedious when the driving later moved toward its second week.

Our turn north off the Road came when we went to Strongsville, Ohio, to see what we could find out about Cully's family who had settled that area many years earlier. The link to Anna would be there, too, I thought, and the trip thus took on a double purpose.

It was a little town up toward Cleveland and it took us a while to reach there. It had well ordered streets with a large town green and a church and town hall, a school that looked new, and quite a few stores and filling stations. A man at one of the filling stations directed us to the town clerk's office at the lower end of the green, and we went there just before noon.

Richard Wentworth was the town clerk and he helped us find the records which showed that John Culbertson had owned a small piece of land with his brother and then one day deeded it over to his brother and vanished from the records. That must have been when he moved further west. The brothers had bought the land from a Gilbert Strong, great-grandson of one of the town's first settlers, and it was that connection to Anna's family that was the link to why they had moved here.

It also was a hint that for John, the land may have been as much a reason to marry this particular young woman as his love for her herself. That was a dark thought that I did not enjoy thinking, but it did offer a possible explanation for his insistence that they make the initial move west, and an explanation as to why she had changed in her thinking and returned to her home.

But why had she left Cully behind? Was that the demand that John had imposed? Was that the price of her freedom from his iron determination to succeed in the face of repeated poor crops, numerous loans that went unrepaid—the records also showed this—and the mounting despair that his failed dream had undoubtedly wrought upon the family?

These records did not say. They were objective, giving only the names and figures, dates and deeds, agreements and lawsuits. But this quick study seemed certainly to say that the promised land had ceased to hold golden hope for either of them and had, instead, become a bitter and divisive fact in their marriage.

I drove Cully out the road to the address which the records had listed as the Culbertson place, but he did not recognize it and when puzzled strangers answered our knock and said they knew nothing, we did not stay.

We had one more stop to make, a stop recommended by Mr. Wentworth. It was the town library, just off the green. There, he said, was a set of books which told the story of the founding and growth of Strongsville and gave a detailed family tree of the Strong family back to its first patriarch in Massachusetts.

The lives of the Strongs were detailed and fascinating, including generals, teachers, doctors, merchants, and ne'er-do-wells; and the founding of Strongsville in 1816 testified to a life of tremendous energy and strength of spirit of many in the family who came to the Connecticut Western Reserve and began to shape it into a community, including becoming involved in the Wayne, Medina and Cuyahoga Turnpike Road Company.

Soon I located what I had believed was there, a discovery which was an exhilarating surprise even though it said much that I had by now partly expected to find. It was on a page much further on, in a listing of a separate branch of the family, that I found Anna in an enumeration of the children of Harlan and Hannah Elliott Strong.

Anna was the third of five children, the others all male: Robert, Elan, Anna, then Matthew, and the fifth, the youngest, was a boy named Augustus Jared who, in the simple language of the book, had simply "disappeared" one August afternoon at the age of seven. It said no more, yet again, like the time Cully mentioned the name "Strong," it was like a lightning bolt in my brain and heart.

We stayed that night in the home of Philip and Harriet Luce just a block off the town green which they called the Common, and despite the fine room and their excellent dinner, I did not rest well. Thoughts drove through my head, hints linked to mysteries bound by suppositions.

I reached a conclusion which brought such mixed emotions that I lay awake well into the night trying to puzzle out its possibilities. The name Strong, which I seemed to recognize deep in my lost recollections; the odd and vague remembrances of the town names of Connecticut; the similarity of the ages of Augustus and myself, and the increasingly strong wonder whether his "disappearance" and my being placed onto the orphan train were linked. All this led me to surmise on the flimsiest and most circumstantial evidence that the undescribed "disappearance" had been mine and that maybe I was or had been, in fact, Augustus Jared Strong. These were conclusions too swirling to allow an easy sleep.

I was frustrated by my inability to remember. Surely a boy can remember things when he is six. Yet all I was able to see in my mind was a small room and hours spent being sick—in what way I did not know—and a person, a woman, bringing me food and then taking me to another person, and the train, the trip west, and the children lining up on the station platform where Mrs. Anderson spoke with me and asked if I would like to come home with her and be an Anderson. After that, I remembered it all; before that, nothing.

I did not want to believe truly in the tenuous links between my story and that of Augustus Jared Strong, for that would forever change my hopes about Anna, erase a fantasy dream which, with each day, I had come to count on more and more; but it would also mean that Cully and I were returning to the same home. I thought about it from that moment on, and this concentration on it made it appear more and more plausible and almost inevitably true, yet it was so uncertain that I resolved not to tell Cully my thoughts.

It was, I inwardly knew, a case of thinking about something for so long that it became a fact. And Anna? That was true of her as well. I had become very good at turning imagination into reality, and although it made me feel young and invigorated, it also made me feel weak and foolish.

No. None of this was to be shared with Cully.

THIRTY YEARS EARLIER . . . II

The Room

Part 1

The yellow glare slanted in slashing streaks across the midnight wall: light . . . dark . . . light . . . dark. The light was a sharp set of yellow-white bars whose image lasted even after deep night came and the room was dark again, an afterglow vibrating on the wall like remembered moonlight.

He lay amid the moaning and crying, watching the light streaks on the wall, his head throbbing from the bruise at his hairline just above his left eye. Light . . . dark . . . light . . . dark. A child's voice from across the small stifling room cried out suddenly, almost a scream, and then was muffled again in whimpering. He watched the light come on, go off, in endless bursts of luminous stripes on the night wall. And still the many-voiced whimpering and moaning.

Beneath the thin floor he heard music, loud laughing, many men's raucous voices, the sounds of glass on glass. Above him, nothing, the dark, the dim reflections of the light from the wall. Behind his head, facing upward on the thin and straw-filled rough fabric of the pillow, he heard scurrying in the wall, tiny rat feet scampering to search for food, for prey, oblivious to the sounds below or the crying within the room.

The light from the outside BAR sign slashed continually, coldly into the dark and frightening room and he felt sick again. His forehead pounded and he sweated under the coarse blanket. He turned his head and in the bar-lighted moments could see other cots, forms hunched up, some thrashing as dark shapes seething in the small room. Another crying out; another moaning. And down below the loud talk and laughter, and in the wall the rat-feet scurrying. It froze him to silence.

He knew where he was. He could not remember how he got there, but he knew that this was Hell and he was being punished, although he could not remember why. He felt something dash across his legs and he thrashed suddenly in desperate reaction.

Outside the door he heard voices, women's voices, loud whispers strong with anger, arguing.

"He's not goin' to stay there!" said one, a husky, low voice like someone speaking through a heavy towel.

"He is, too! Even dead he'll be worth somethin'. Leave him be!" This was a sharp voice, a stabbing voice ready to scold.

"I'm takin' him out!" There was the sound of a hand on the door knob, a key turned, a tall crack of light from the hall, then the door pulled shut again with a thud and the light went out.

"What'll you do with him?" laughed the sharp other. "You goin' t' keep him? Try to say he's yours?"

"I'm not tellin' you, Mary Manley, so you can snatch him back again and get a dollar for his corpse. But I'm takin' him!" There was a silence.

"So, go on then, and see what trouble it brings you. I'm done with it. Take him if you want, but first you pay me," said the sharp voice angrily. "Good riddance. And go down the back way so Keegan don't see you or we'll both get clubbed. You get me in trouble with this and I'll skin you!"

"Good, Mary," soothed the husky voice. "It'll be fine. Just say he must have got up in the night and run off."

"I'll do," snapped the other, "but make it quick." And he heard the sound of feet on the stairs, vanishing.

The key again ground in the hard lock, the doorknob creaked, and in the dim slant light of the open door he saw a large woman come in. The door shut. Then a hand touched him and he shrank back.

"There, now, boy, don't be afraid," whispered the husky voice. He smelled cigarette smoke. "You're gettin' out of this damned place. Don't make any sound." There were surryings in the wall again, and she instinctively slapped the wall behind his head and it was quiet. They listened for noise, and downstairs the loud sounds went on.

She pulled him up to sitting, the mattress crackling, and his head throbbed. He felt his arms being put into sleeves, pants started on his legs, and he was lifted into a standing position and the pants tugged up and buttoned at his waist.

In the dark he was close to her now, surrounded by her, and he smelled also the ironing smell of scorched cloth. He still could not see her except in the flashes of the bar-sign light, and even then he could not see her face for she was bent, her black coarse hair like a hiding shawl down around her face. But he felt her strong hands helping him get dressed and said nothing.

"Ah, you're still burnin' with some fever," she said as her hand touched his cheek. "Come on now, and no noise. We're goin' where you'll get well and get some food. Shhhhhhhh, now. Can you walk?"

He tried, took a step or two in the dark. "Naw. Here," she whispered, and put her large hands on his waist and hoisted him up, almost over her shoulder. "Quiet, now."

He knew the door was open again and now saw it behind him, receding, and then saw the top of it vanishing on the upper floor as he went down, closer to the loud voices and music and laughing, then turned away from that, too, catching a moment of light and then steps down again, another door, and suddenly into the hot and noisy street air of the city's summer night.

She did not talk again nor ask him if he wanted to try to walk. She hurried, walking rapidly, saying nothing, carrying her bundle through people who did not turn to look as they passed by them. Turned up another street, quieter, darker. Turned again, crossed over, several more blocks on black streets past dark doorways at the tops of stone-steps, in a door, up some stairs, a landing, more stairs, and into a flat. She pulled the chain of a small lamp.

She carried him into the next room to a bed and carefully set him down, lifted his legs up onto the bed, drew a blanket over him. "Rest for a minute," she said. "I'll get you somethin'." And she went into the next room without closing the door.

He heard the sounds of cabinets, dishes, the thunk of an ice box door. Then she was back. "Here," she said, still speaking softly. "Milk and a piece of bread. We'll get you somethin' more in the mornin'."

He sat up on the edge of the bed with her help and swallowed a long drink of the cool milk, then nibbled on the bread like a squirrel. He tried to remember when he had last had food and could not. She looked at his bruised forehead, left, and returned with a warm, wet cloth and sponged it off, touching the spot gently, watching him for pain.

"There," she said. "You got some bump. They said you were knocked out. You remember?"

"No," he said, and touched the bruise lightly with his fingers. No, he did not remember. The room smelled like dry wood.

She did not understand at first that it wasn't just the bump he could not remember. It was everything. "Look," she said. "You've been pretty sick, love, and now we're goin' to try to get you right. It'll take a few days, but if you rest and eat, you'll get better." She looked straight into his eyes and he believed her. "You'll be all right now. But you wouldn't 've made it back there in that sick room and they would have liked that."

She set something in order on the far side of the room, straightened a small braided rug with her foot, then stood looking at him. "You understand, I may go out some, but you stay inside until I say, or they'll likely spot you again and snatch you back, you hear?" He nodded. "Then we'll help you get goin' right again. There you go," she said, taking the empty glass from his small hand, "you lie back now and finish your bread and get some sleep. I'll be in there on the couch," she said, motioning with her head towards the next room, "and there's nothin' to worry about. You're safe now. Just get some sleep."

He wondered who she was and about the other sick children back in that hellish room above the noise. Then, with just a small light showing steadily in the next room, he soundly slept.

Part 2

After many days he was better. A woman in a green dress carrying a briefcase had been to see him twice and said he was a fine-looking boy and she had decided he could go with her to find a good home. These events were a mystery to him. Why he was here was a mystery to him. How he got here was a mystery. He tried to remember a time before the Hell room, but the pieces did not fit to make a memory. They were just odd sounds, odd images, without the story memory should have.

The husky-voiced woman he now called Mrs. Kate had tended his bruise and fed him regularly, and he was walking steadily again, even twice going out onto the hot street with Mrs. Kate when she went for groceries. When she was at work "making clothes," she said, he stayed inside and watched the street below through the hot window, leaning out to catch the breeze when there was one, watching people.

He asked few questions and received even fewer answers. The other children in that dark room probably were dying, he now knew, and when he asked why Mrs. Kate had taken him out, she spoke vaguely about someone named Timmy who had been lost. When he thought of the dark room he thought of something rotting, a heavy, solid stench that lay upon the beds with the whimpering children and weighed them down.

He spent days at the window letting the sun strike his face when it passed between the buildings for a while each day. It was warm and heated his skin and felt good, a feeling that was inward as well as on his face and arms, a sound and even a taste of goodness. He faced up into the sun and closed his eyes and the sun warmed his eyelids and cheeks, and it entered him and made him stronger.

On the sill of the other window in his room, two sparrows had built their nest, wedging it into the corner against the wall, fixing it carefully with some mud. They had brought scraps of string, hair, twigs, strips of paper, even a shoelace, and, like small instinctive carpenters, had woven themselves a safe nest in which to lay their eggs. He had his chair in place and each day watched.

When one snuggled into the nest and laid her eggs, the three brown ovals soon cracked and released their strange looking bits of feathered life. And the baby birds grew, fed by their parents' returns with tiny bugs and choice morsels much as Mrs. Kate had brought food to him. And when the baby birds had grown and were fully feathered, they flew, and he knew that he would, too, when Mrs. Kate was ready to have him go.

In the evenings, after their meal together, Mrs. Kate read to him. But when she realized that he, too, could read, she knew the books she had were far too young for him. She came back the next day from a junk shop, and they read together in the evenings after that, enjoying the tales Peter Rabbit, Uncle Wiggley, and Mr. Toad.

In the daytime when she was at work, he sat down with the books again, looking into the illustrations turning rabbits and toads and moles into little people with jackets and hats and eye glasses. Then he even imagined a huge person named Keegan, like the giant stomping after Jack, clubbing people. "I'll grind his bones to make my bread!" shouted the deep, rough voice somewhere back in the other dark. But he, like Jack, had found the beanstalk and gotten away.

The third time the woman in green came he was told her name was Mrs. Palcher and he knew it was time to leave. He trusted her because he had come to love Mrs. Kate. His clothes had been washed during the night and were ready for him that morning. Mrs. Kate held him tightly in her arms and kissed him over and over on the forehead. "Timmy would be very happy," she said, and brought her handkerchief up to her mouth as tears slid down her cheeks. "Good luck," she said. "I know you will find a good home." And then, to Mrs. Palcher she said, "Take special care of him, please do."

"I will," said Mrs. Palcher, and they went down the stairs and out into the hot and busy city street jostling with noise.

It wasn't that he did not want to leave, but he feared not knowing what was next. He had hugged Mrs. Kate a long time. Then they left.

"Where are we going?" he asked.

"First to the office, then to the train station, and then . . . to a new life for you. Don't worry, I will be with you all the way. I'll take good care of you. And you'll meet new friends along the way and will be chosen by a fine family to live with."

He walked in his smaller steps beside her, looking at the street doorways and shops, turning once to look back toward Mrs. Kate's wooden building but he could not tell which one it was, could not see any difference between one doorway and another, tried to find his window but could not and saw that several windows had nests in the corners. When they turned the corner, the street was gone forever.

"You have not told us your name," she said, almost as a question. "They'll need to know your name before we can send you on the train because they want to have very good records. Can you say your name for me?"

He looked at her and wanted to say it, but he could not remember it and thought it would be wrong to make one up. He knew he must have a name, but it was gone, like the doorway, and he stopped walking and just looked at Mrs. Palcher, wondering why he could not remember his name.

She thought it was just that he would not tell her, and she said, "We'll have to give you one then, won't we? We will call you John and you are . . . let me look at you . . . you are six years old, I'd say." She studied him and saw the puzzlement in his face. "That's all right. John is a good name and many of the boys we get have that name. Some of them spell it differently, depending on what country they have come from, but it's a good name. John, then. All right?"

He nodded, not knowing what else to do, and started walking with her again. They turned another corner and came onto a street where the sun shone directly onto the whole length of the street. It was warm, there was a little breeze on this street, and someone had planted a box of red flowers beside the red brick doorway which they entered. Above the double doors was a large curved sign like a half-moon, with gold letters trimmed in black on a white background: Children's Aid Society.

"Here we are," she said. "Come on, John, there's a whole new world waiting for you."

They went down a hallway that seemed very long, into an office that had a door with a slanted pane of glass open above it.

"Here he is," said Mrs. Palcher. "This is John," and took him to a straight-backed wooden chair next to a large brown desk. When he sat he looked at the man at the desk who was hidden behind stacks of papers and folders.

"Hello, young man," said the man. "Let's fill out your card and then get you on your way." The man swung in his chair and looked at the large round clock on the wall, turned to Mrs. Palcher and said, "Just in time. We've got less than an hour. You go ahead to the station and see that everything is all right."

Mrs. Palcher patted the boy's shoulder and said, "It will be all right, John. Mr. Brace will bring you to the station and I'll see you again on the train. OK? You'll be all right. Don't worry."

In fact he was empty of worry. The room of dying, the being carried out in the night, the flight through the streets, the days with Mrs. Kate, leaving again with Mrs. Palcher, this new place and stranger writing down a name for him. It was just happenings, events, almost as if it were not about him, rapid moments of pain and fear and sickness and sunlight and sparrows and milk. And now, a train. Someone came and pinned a name tag onto his shirt; another person measured him and checked his teeth and hands; a third put some powder into his hair and tousled it around, then toweled him off; still another took him to a room with clothing in it, selected a set of clothes for him, wrote on the bag "JOHN, 6", put the clothes inside it, folded the top shut, and gave him the bag to carry to the station.

The man who had been at the desk then led him outside again, and he climbed up into an old green bus that said Children's Aid Society on the side. Inside there were other children, but they were quiet. When the bus started, someone cried in the back of the bus, but he was sitting in the front and did not look around. He watched the traffic, the other busses and trucks and cars and wagons and carts, the yellow trolleys clanging down the middle, people moving up and down the sidewalks and across in front of them, people calling out things they wanted to sell, a man with fish, a man with a cart mounded with rags.

The green bus labored its slow way through this maze, turned a last corner, swung into a huge stone entrance-way just for cars and busses, a towering, gray, arched entrance. Three people, a man and two women, came toward the bus, the driver opened the door and said toward the back, "Don't forget your bag of clothes," and told them to get off and stand there until everyone was out.

They stood there waiting, looking at everyone else as the bus pulled away. He saw that he was not the smallest one, but there were many bigger. He saw that there were girls as well as boys.

"Let's go, and stay together!" said the man, and they went under the archway that smelled of old stones and cool dampness and shade, down a long flight of steps under a gleaming vast skylight, down another flight, and onto a platform that stretched deep into the black cavern of the station. There were already many other boys and girls with tan paper bags waiting to get on a steaming, hissing train with dark green passenger cars. He did not see Mrs. Palcher.

He was told to board the train and, once he made it up the difficult iron steps, he was told to hand his bag to the person just inside the train's doorway. "Just find a seat anywhere," said the person. "One child to a seat. Boys this way, girls that." He did, and soon the train jolted, then started to roll smoothly into the blackness of the cavern.

CHAPTER 28

Cully

Usually we do not travel but to go to a farm and come back, so this trip will be a new kind and Doc says it will take a week at least.

His car is comfortable and smells like a good car, brown smells and earth smells and a little liniment, just the way it was the first time. There's dust on the dashboard and in the little shelves beneath the round clock and speedometer. The steering wheel is the same blue as the car, but the seats are gray and smooth and soft. Our suitcases are in the trunk because he saved the back seat for me to sleep on if I get tired.

He has a map and tells me what the route will be, but I don't know most of the places he names and just follow it by trying to follow the red line on the map that is our road. Some times we go on blue lines, and the numbers of the routes show that we are making a steady ride east.

We stay at night in cabins when we can find them, which is most of the time. Doc drives up to a house with a sign out, and then he goes in and rents a cabin or a room for us for the night. The cabins are little houses with a bed and a place to wash. None of them have kitchens or porches.

One night we cannot find a place and keep driving until well after dark. It is somewhere in Ohio, I think, and the road is narrow, with a line in the center to keep cars apart. When a car comes, its lights are bright until it puts them down, and then it is easier to see where the road is.

This road goes through woods and each side of the road is black with no houses, only trees in the night. We are driving along in this black tunnel and Doc suddenly says, "Look!" and up ahead on the side is what looks like a big paper bag standing beside the road. It is tan and brown and white, and seems firm.

Then it moves as we get closer and it starts to walk into the road and then back. Doc has to slow down. Then it hunches down a bit and starts to fly, and it has long, brown, big wings that flap slowly to lift its heavy owl body off the ground. It is flying in the same direction we are going but it stays only about four feet off the ground, flying right along the edge of the road, its great dark powerful wings moving slowly in a rhythm that lifts it steadily forward.

It does not seem to be trying to get away and it does not veer off or rise up. Slowly we are catching up to it. I roll down the window and am on my knees on the seat so's I can see better, and I can hear the swoosh, swoosh of its huge wings. The owl is now just ahead of the fender and going almost our speed, or else Doc has slowed down. It does not look back at us and does not seem to fear the car that it must know is right there off its shoulder. The car lights have shown us every feather working as it moves its wings, and now we come up along side it and it is flying right beside me just even with my window! I hear it and even smell it, the soft bird-feathery smell like the hawk's feather. I can see its eyes and its round face with the circular rings of feathers, and I think it looks at me once, too.

We keep going side by side for what seems a long time, but now I think it was one of those slowed down moments again and was really only a few seconds. But I see him so well! If I wanted, I could reach out and touch him. My face is outside the window and is just a few feet from his, and he still just keeps flapping his gigantic wings and flying right beside us, as if he had been waiting for us and now is joining us. His wings just about brush the side of the car in their up and down swings and the motion-wind from them reaches me. It is the most amazing and exciting thing I have ever seen and I cannot stop watching him.

It is as if he knew that we could not rise up in the car and fly beside him up there, so he comes down to the road level and flies beside us for a while. He was *waiting* for us beside the road.

That is the night that the owl became my favorite bird, and when I have the chance I start reading all I can about them. I even start to think that that owl knew who I was and liked flying beside me that night. I know now that it was not ordinary owl behavior. They do not do that.

CHAPTER 29

Doc

The Road looks straight, or nearly so, on a map. The one we had from the flying red horse of the Mobil Oil Company showed a fine red-line route stretching flatly east and west. In fact, we spent more time on grades and hills than on flats, and far more time on curves than on straight-aways.

Yet the beauty of the early summer countryside was undeniable, and the contours, so drastically different from our home area, kept us ever entertained with new vistas and visual challenges. Rivers, hills, ravines, and forests taught us both about the diverse aspects of the land; and our descent into Wheeling, West Virginia, was as exciting as any part of the Road, only to be followed by the climb up again, taxing the car and causing Cully to wonder if there were a hill somewhere which did not end.

Most of the covered bridges had been replaced with metal spans, and hardly a hint of the famous "S" bridges remained on the Road, the ones where the road approached the stream at an angle, but the crossing had been built at right angles to the stream; then the road on the other side angled away again. The route, in growing, had been cleansed of some of these classic old aspects which had become nuisances in the faster age but which might some day be part of its lore and its romanticized past. One feature which had survived the improvements was the "Y" bridge in Zanesville, perhaps the only place in the nation, if not the world, where three roads fork high above a river. Cully enjoyed that bridge so much we stopped on the far side and walked back onto it to see for ourselves.

It is well that Cully was a quiet sort, for now, especially now, I was not a talkative traveling companion as I pondered the various possibilities and tried to discern which was the truth. These thoughts completely filled my mind, and I often found that I had driven many hours with little recollection of the scenes we had passed. Cully held the wrinkled and softening map and was good at alerting me to what towns lay ahead, but beyond that he watched out the window, and for me much of this part of the trip elapsed as if I had been unconscious.

Anna. Lovely, musical Anna who had left her son behind and gone home.

Always there were two thoughts in my mind when I thought of Anna. One was the image which I had conjured up almost from the first mention of her name, as one forms visual pictures of people long before meeting them, pictures drawn from impressions, the sound of a voice, a reputation, a phrase someone has said. This image in Anna's case was beautiful and perfect, a melodious voice, and an understanding heart which blended to create a perfect woman.

The other was the ravenous, nagging awareness that the truth would be less pleasing, that she was now considerably older than the Anna in the picture, that she had abandoned her son, that the farm years had undoubtedly had an effect on her view of life and its possibilities, that there was not much likelihood that she trusted in the potential for joy and love enduring in any relationship between a man and a woman. This Anna would not regard me as anything more than someone who conducted Cully home. Even her own journey might not stimulate for her a sense of the time and distance to which we had committed ourselves simply to find her.

In truth there was the third thought, the one I feared yet which was the most intriguing of all: was I really Augustus? Could I possibly be Anna's brother? Then what a tangle my mind went into and I saw again the maze into which I was driving, knowing no answers, no certainties.

I had to know one fact from Cully, and somewhere in eastern Pennsylvania I finally forced the words out after we had crossed a large river: "When you wrote to your mother, did you tell her about where you had been living since your Pa died?" Even as I strung out this elaborate question, I knew that what I was really asking was "Did you tell her about me?"

"I told her that I was living with Doc Anderson ever since Pa died," he said.

What a wonderfully innocent answer. It told me nothing. "No," I wanted to say, "I mean did you tell her about *me* ?" But I did not venture to ask that immodest and crucial question, and so, approached the destination as a stranger.

There were questions that spun annoyingly in my mind, refusing to leave even after I had repeated to myself the final postponing statement that I would simply have to go see.

Yet even that was not a moment I welcomed. Could we find her? We should have waited for a response from the magistrate in Tolland, but we had left before one arrived, if he had even sent one.

I knew that I would need to figure out a way to raise the subject without stating it as a fact, because it might not be a fact and then my "return" would seem a sham, a cruel trick designed to deceive the family for some personal and nefarious reason.

But how had I gotten on that orphan train and why?

Day after day these questions filled my mind, days of nearly unremembered driving, nights of uneasy, sleepless sleep.

My nervousness did not become noticeable until one day we turned onto a fine highway adorned with beautifully sculpted overpasses, and I knew that it was not days any longer but merely hours until this part of the road—a finely kept, toll-booth-dotted portion called the Merritt Parkway—would deliver us to Hartford and, from there we would take state roads to Tolland and find out the Magistrate and what he knew.

The closeness to our goal had not eased my mind, had not softened the meaning of the word "home" into a hearth-warmed childhood memory. It was now a dilemma with choices leading to good and bad at every turn.

From Hartford, an exit onto a winding, tarred state route 74, and a stark black-and-white sign reading: "Tolland 24 miles."

CHAPTER 30

Cully

We have crossed so many rivers on this trip that I can't count them. It starts in the state of Indiana and goes on ever since. They seem to be getting bigger, too, and when we go across the river near New York City, Doc calls it the Hudson River, that was the biggest one of all.

Doc tells me the story of Henry Hudson, how he was sailing to try to find new ways to China and got lost and his men got mad at him and set him off in a small boat. Down below us the river is very wide, and a small white boat is moving up river, its V-shaped path widening behind it for a long way. I can see two people on the boat, and they look very small from up here in the middle of that wide river.

"Why'd they do that?" I ask Doc.

"He wanted to go on. He was trying to find a passage through to the Orient. They thought he'd led them into a dead end, a gigantic bay with no way out except the way they came in and no hope of discovering anything or finding riches. Then Arctic winter came and the ship got trapped in the ice and they had to survive the bitter cold before they could get away. They were tired, hungry, angry, some of them sick. Even scared. It was a huge bay up north, north of Canada. It is way above the top of your map. So they took over and set him adrift in a boat."

"And did what then?"

"Headed home."

"Without a captain?"

"There always are many men on a boat who can sail it, if it comes to that. But it is called a 'mutiny' when the crew takes over. That's what happened when the winter ice broke and the ship was free to sail again."

"Wasn't it mean to put him out? Wouldn't he die?"

"It was mean, but they did not do it all at once. They thought that their reasons were good. Their fears and concerns must have been growing for many weeks, and this was just the moment when they couldn't take any more. He must have said 'no' one more time and that was it. I guess they wanted to go home; he wanted to find China."

We are across the river now and turn around a curve to get onto a very fine road that soon has trees in the center.

"Did he have food? Could he get to shore?"

"No. I don't think so. It is a wide, wide sea more than a bay, way up north, and even though the ice had broken and it was early summer, I doubt that he survived."

"Nobody knows what happened to him?"

"Nobody."

"Was he alone?"

Doc seems to wait for a minute before he tells me. "No. His young son was put off with him. I think there were some sailors, too, maybe six or seven, who stayed loyal to him. None were ever heard from again."

"His son? Why his son?"

"I don't know," he says, and looks over at me.

We are headed into beautiful woods and forest on the fine road. Doc is usually very quiet, but the story about Henry Hudson bothers me, not just because of the boy but that's the big reason. He must have been scared when they made him leave the ship in a small boat on the huge sea. I wonder if he cried. I wonder if his father could do anything to help them. I wonder why his father took him on the boat at all. It seems that traveling that way isn't something a boy should be asked to do. He should have been at home with his mother. Maybe he couldn't be.

It still is sad to think of the boy just disappearing like that. "Nobody knows," Doc says. I bet his name was John. I hope he had something with him, some toy, maybe, that he liked.

Most of the time Doc is quiet while he drives, and I am, too. There's so much to see, and usually I just look at it and try to see deep into the woods or houses and see what's going on far back from the road.

I don't know why I started asking about the Hudson River. I wonder if every river has a story behind it as sad as that one. Doc says it's interesting that a man who failed to find what he was looking for should end up with a river and a bay named after him. I guess other people felt sorry for him and his son, too.

151

The towns we pass through are not like Weed, where everything is spread out and the houses have fields between them. These houses are closer and they are almost all white, and the little groups they form seem cozy and safer than where houses are far apart. In between them are not fields but woods, usually. Some of the houses have garages, even barns and chicken coops, and some have dog houses.

At times there are many other cars on the road and now and then a horse-drawn wagon with hay being moved from one place to another. The new hay crop can't be ready yet, I know, so this must be someone buying hay until his comes in.

Then there are parts of the road where we don't see any cars for miles and miles, and these are usually the parts where there aren't many houses either.

We cross another river the next afternoon and Doc tells me what it is and later writes it down for me. It's the "Connecticut." I tell him I can spell it and he says, "Go ahead," so I do and he is very pleased. He says it's an Indian word that means "long river." So they were here once and now they're gone, too. And now there is a big city where they used to live. I look on the map and can see lots of strange words like Connecticut. They must be Indian words.

The city is Hartford, the map says, and I ask Doc if that is an Indian word, too.

"No," he says. "I think it is a combination of two words. 'Hart' means a deer, a male deer, and 'ford' is a place in the river where you can cross because the river is shallower there. So this must be a place where the water is shallow and deer could cross the river. Maybe," he says with a smile and then he shrugs.

I remember Hartford later because of the posters and just outside it there is a place where the road swings back and forth across a single pair of railroad tracks. The road here is not a wide highway, and as we drive along it, a small three-car train goes along and we have to keep slowing down or stopping for it when we get to a place where the road crosses the tracks again. It is going slowly, just an engine and coal car and a flat car with some kind of machines on it, but it is a heavy load and the smoke booms out of the smokestack in black clouds that show how hard it is working, even on the flat.

Because of the curvy road we can't go fast either, so we stay with the train a long time, maybe ten minutes or more, and first we are on its left side and then on its right. It is an odd way to plan a road.

Doc sees it before I do, the white sign with black letters that says "Tolland" and has a little black arrow pointing straight up. I know it means straight ahead, but it looks funny to see it pointing into the sky.

Soon we will be there. Maybe another hour. This is the twelfth day of our trip and I am excited that it is almost over and I will see Ma again.

CHAPTER 31

Doc

The trip east of Hartford passed through acres of white-tented fields, land where tobacco grows under the protective cover of gauze sheets held up by many posts. It was an unusual sight for someone used to the open plains and flat fields of southern Illinois, reminding the traveler of winding sheets and burials on the one hand, and of sun-up to sun-down work by people who gain scant reward for their labor on the other. Nevertheless, it was a beautiful land. Its clear air made the green woods rich and luxuriant, the soil was dark and fertile, and large healthy herds grazed on stone-walled hillsides and riverside meadows.

Route 74 rolled through green woods, an old route leading from small town to small town, near lakes, repeating the clear and rural image again and again. Indian names on the road signs merged into names taken from England, names of first settlers, names of the terrain: Skunamaug River, Manchester, Rocky Hill, Bolton Notch, Talcottville, New Britain.

Here and there on a telephone pole or the side of a building, nailed to a wooden fence or projecting through a store-front window was a bright red, white, and blue poster advertising a week-long circus coming to Hartford, and it was but a matter of time before Cully's curiosity and desire melded into a request to "go see the circus." He had never been close to anything like that, and the idea of animals doing tricks had him in a spell. Of course my answer was yes, for I know that we will be only an hour from Hartford and could easily satisfy this delight in him even while still seeking the answers for which we have traveled so far.

In fact, it was a pleasure to think of stopping, living somewhere, and doing things that settled families do.

We swung down a long curving hill road and rose gently between two stone walls into the town of Tolland, with a sign indicating when it was first settled and what the population is.

It was almost like arriving in Strongsville once again, for the New England influence which established the central green or Common in Strongsville was simply a retaining of the same tradition from these older towns. This Common here was long, stretching perhaps a quarter mile or more, dissected across the middle by the road which slashed through and continued east.

There was the town clerk's office, there were the churches, the jail, many clean and sober homes; there arched the maple trees and elms over the small general store, the school, the library. And there, too, was the small courthouse, the building where we hoped to find the magistrate. Its plaque named the building and told of the man who was honored by having the courthouse named for him.

We parked in front where they had some logs to make cars keep off the lawn, and it wasn't until I turned off the motor that I heard the zizzling sound. The engine was hot, almost boiling over, and small filaments of steam curled out through the slots in the side of the hood and vanished. "I'm going to raise the hood while we're in there," I said, ". . . let the motor cool down a bit."

I cannot describe the throbbing in my heart as we ascended the steps to enter the court building, an inner beating so hard and loud it surely must have been visible in my face and audible to anyone on the street.

The sweet-smelling wooden hallway was quiet; three or four doors, all closed. The names were on each door and finally, with no more said than a whispered "There it is," we came to Judge Caldword's office and stood still in front of the reddish wood of his chambers' entrance, both knowing that all the miles of traveling meant nothing now and that here, upon entering this room, the past would end and our new lives would begin.

I nodded to Cully and let out a breath of nervousness, then knocked.

"Come in," said a woman's voice. The brass knob turned silently, and I held it firmly as I opened the door and motioned for Cully to step in first. I followed and closed the door.

The office seemed vast and ceremonial, with high ceilings, tall windows, and official flags and certificates hanging on the walls. Brightness on one side fading into dim corners. Against an inner wall was a large oak roll-top desk on which were set several tidy stacks of papers and whose pigeon holes swelled with papers jutting into the space above the desk's writing surface. At one end of the desk, on a pull-out shelf, was a large black Underwood typewriter.

"May I help you?" she asked as we stood still for too long. She was near the desk with a few pages of something in her hand, apparently heading toward a filing cabinet across the room. Her smile was efficient, not unfriendly, and designed to get an answer.

"Yes," I said. "I am Gunnar Anderson and this is John Culbertson. I wrote to Judge Caldword several weeks ago asking for his aid in locating someone. Is it possible to see him?"

"Oh, I am so sorry. The Judge is not in his chambers today," she said. "He is on vacation for a week and will not return until next Tuesday."

It is possible to become so engrossed with one's own plans and desires that the rest of the world must surely be aware of them and ready to respond to them. Travel all this way and the one person who is able to direct us further is simply not available. I had not even considered that possibility.

"You should have called first," she smiled.

I did not know what to do. Cully's look was asking me, and I could not think what to do next. It was like arriving at a dead end. We could not simply sit still until the judge returned, even if there were the finest lodgings available. Our expectations were too strong, our need for some result from our long journey pounded on us and forbade that we now stand still for nearly as long. But what else was there to do?

The answer was obvious and Cully again spoke with the sure and precise question which would restart our apparently stalled search: "Do you know where my mother lives?"

"Your mother?" The woman's focus now was entirely on Cully and, although she glanced at me from time to time in the next few minutes, it was to Cully and his desire to find his mother that she spoke.

"What is your mother's name?"

"Anna Strong Culbertson. Only she's just Anna Strong again now," he said.

I did not doubt what he said, but it came as a surprise to me and I may have said "What?" softly to him, because he looked at me and said, "She changed it back. That's why the magistrate knows her." Dr. Anderson, the famed scientific mind, had never asked that question.

"Yes, I know Anna Strong," she said cheerily. It was a moment of sunlight bursting into the room. "That is, I know who she is. I don't know her personally very well. But I was a witness when she came in and requested that her maiden name be restored by Judge Caldword. We spoke a bit at that time. Very nice woman. Attractive. She is your mother?"

"Yes, ma'm. We were in Illinois when she came back home, and then my father died one day and Doc and I have come to look for her."

Her quick "is that true?" glance my way caused me to nod. Yes, it was true. "You poor dear," she cooed to Cully. "You've traveled all this way, and now you don't know where she lives. Is that what the Judge was going to help you with?"

"Yes, m'am. We hope so."

"How long have you been on the road?"

"Almost two weeks," he said.

"From Illinois?"

"Yes," he said.

"My stars! I hardly know where Illinois is. I've never been west of Poughkeepsie. What a long trip you've had!"

She turned to her desk and set her pages down at last, neatly, went to an open-shelf file on the far wall beneath a portrait of Lincoln, and brought out a large, flat book that she carried past us and set down gently on a brown heavy-legged table beneath the windows.

It was an odd-looking black book, wider than it was tall, obviously weighty because she used both hands to carry it, with a purple ribbon emerging from a certain page and lapping down the front. On the old and slightly marred cover was a gold shield or coat-of-arms, an ornate and gleaming dragon within and extending beyond the borders of the shield, front claws raised, fiery tongue sensing the air. Beneath, some words that may have been in Latin but appeared to be finely shaped and almost Oriental.

She swung open the cover and started looking in the upper corners of pages for some sign of what she wanted, carefully turning the stiff but thin pages as if they were dried tissue paper. "Here it is," she said. "Come over here and I'll show you the way."

We eagerly walked over to the open book, its pages made bright by the sunlight slanting through the high windows. It was a book of maps of parts of Connecticut.

She was bent over the book, but she straightened, turned to us, and held out her hand. "My name is Lake, by the way. Forgive me for not introducing myself sooner but I got caught up in your story. Enid Lake." She held out her hand to each of us in a delicate, soft gesture, and we shook her finger tips. "This will help you. See here?

Here is where you are now," and she pointed politely with a pencil. "I'll show you on the maps first and then we'll write it out so that you can find your way. Lord," she said softly, "all the way from Illinois."

What she indicated was a winding road that passed by little squares for houses, some of them clustered near where the road crossed a hatched pair of lines indicating a railroad, over a river, through a crossroads, past a cemetery.

"There are two hills here," she indicated a place, "well, actually there is one hill. But it levels out and then rises again." On the map was the notation "The Hill."

"You follow that over the crest and down the other side, about a mile I imagine, and then you will be in 'The Hollow.' The Strong house is there," and she lightly drew a small star on the map. "She gazed at Cully who stood staring at the spot. "I think you will find her there."

She returned to her roll-top desk and brought back a pad of paper on which she wrote out the directions we were to follow.

And so, at last, we knew where we were going. "Mrs. Lake, thank you very much for all your trouble," I said. "I am sorry that we did not call to let you know we were coming, but you have done wonderfully in helping us."

"Not at all. It was my pleasure," she said, "and you, John, good luck in finding your mother. I'll bet she has missed you." She raised her hands to her cheeks and again smiled. "Oh, my goodness, I almost forgot," she said, reaching for a blue glass bowl and holding it up toward us. "Would you like a piece of candy?"

I declined, but Cully said "thank you" and took a piece of the hard candy. He turned back and held it up to show me. It was in the shape of an owl.

PART VI

Home Again

Chapter 32

Cully

A kind lady in the magistrate's office shows us how to get to the Strongs' house. She says it is about seven miles away and is over some hills.

People helped us and were very friendly all along the way, and now Mrs. Lake shows us more kindness. She has a big, heavy book with maps in it, and she shows us just where to go to reach the Strongs'.

At times during the trip I was excited, like with the owl, but what I feel now is even more. I feel like I can hardly breathe as we get back into the car and turn down past the jail to continue on our route. It's a sad place, the jail. The front looks like a house painted yellow, but the back is dark bricks and ivy growing over them up to the roof, with small windows with bars, and in one of them a man's face is looking out. He doesn't move as we drive by, and he doesn't see us. He doesn't know how excited I am.

It goes down along a pasture with tan cows grazing, then back around corners and then down a long slope that curves left at the bottom in a wide swing. We cross a little river now, and the sign by it makes my heart jump even faster. It says "Willimantic River" and Doc sees it, too, and grins at me. That's the name on the back of Ma's picture.

After the river there's a railroad platform and a small dark-red station with a ramp. Before the tracks there's a set of crossed white boards on a pole that say "Stop, Look, and Listen." Doc does. Then we bump over the rough tracks. Beyond that is a rise and a crossroads, and a road sign points to the right and says "Willimantic" again. It is a tingly feeling to be so close.

We go straight, up a steep hill and then down into a valley and then up again, and when we flatten out there is a big cemetery on the left side and then we start up again. Right there is a Texaco filling station, and Doc stops to get gas. "It won't do to run out of gas now," he says.

The pumps are the old kind, with a handle to pump and a big glass jar on the top of the pump that fills up with the red gas to the line where you want it, so many gallons, and then you put the hose's nozzle into the gas tank and it drains out of the glass jar and down into the car.

Most of the ones we had seen on the trip were the new kind, with the dial that spins around and hums as the gas goes in. These were set in under a roof so you could get gas and not get wet if it was raining. The big window of the station had signs for oil and I could see a counter inside with candy for sale. Doc pays the man.

When we come to the top of the hill, the road levels off again, and there's the village green with houses around it and two churches. Then we start down the long slope into the small valley. I remember what Mrs. Lake has said. It will be about one mile more.

I start to become frightened because I cannot remember exactly what Ma looks like. I have her in my mind, but I am not sure that that picture is right. What did her voice sound like? How can I not know? How come I can't remember?

We drive down the hill and the woods open up and there is a farm house and a shed back from the road. The driveway is dirt and there's a gray mailbox but it doesn't have a name on it.

"I think this is it," says Doc. "You ready?"

I tell him I am, and he turns into the driveway, bumping down off the road into the hollows that rain has probably made in the dirt.

We pass a catalpa tree and come to the front of the white house, a long veranda at the top of two big stone slabs for steps. The porch pillars are old white and need painting, and they are partly hidden behind big green bushes that look as though no one has cared for them because they are growing into the walk and up onto the porch railing.

No one comes to the door, but a corner of a curtain is pulled aside and then drops back. We go up the stone-slab steps, across the wide veranda, and lift the brass knocker and rap three times on the door. It opens.

"Yes?"

It is a small white-haired woman who asks us, not the person I expect to see. She doesn't know who we are.

"Mrs. Strong?" asks Doc.

"Yes. Can I do something for you?"

"Mrs. Strong, my name is . . ." and then Doc pauses and I look at him and he seems not sure what to say, even though he's only telling his name.

Then he goes on, "My name is Gunnar Anderson and this young man is John Culbertson."

The old woman does not seem to know who that is, and she just looks at us and says, "Yes?" again. Then she looks at me and very softly says my name. "Cully? Is it really you?"

"Yes, m'am, it is," I say, and she puts both her hands over her mouth and says "Oh" as if she can't believe it.

"We've come from Illinois to find Ma. Is Ma here?"

"Oh, Cully, let me have a look at you," she says, and takes both my arms and holds me still while she looks at me. "I can't believe this," she says. "You really came. We did not think you would." She holds one hand in the other and puts a thumbnail between her teeth as if she can't decide. "Yes, your mother is here. She just went down to the chickens to gather eggs. You can go meet her."

She points down the hill toward a pond with a gray wooden building beside it, and past the corner I can see the edge of what might be the chicken coop. "Yes, that's it, you can go down there and surprise her."

I run down the grassy path toward the pond and go carefully around the edge next to the building. Before I can get all the way there, she comes around the corner carrying a metal basket with some eggs in it, and when she sees me she hollers "Cully!" and sets the basket down and runs to me with her arms out.

She holds me tight and is crying, and I know who she is by the smell of her clothes and the strong arms holding me close to her. She kneels down and holds me some more, and I give her a long hug, too, and all I can say is "Ma . . . Ma."

"Oh, look at you. And you've come so far! How big you are! What a big boy! Are you well? Are you hungry? Come up to the house and we'll get you some food. My how you've grown! I hardly recognize you," and she squeezes me again.

Then as we turn around and start back to the house, for the first time she sees Doc. She uses her apron to wipe her tears. "Are you . . . ?" she says, startled.

"I'm Gunnar Anderson, An . . . Miss Strong," he says and holds out his hand, smiling.

CHAPTER 33

Doc

It was one of those relatively short trips which seem to take a very long time, as if desire makes time meaningless and distances endless. It was early afternoon when we left Mrs. Lake and the judge's chambers. The road swung easily around curves and swooped into valleys and up green hills, and then as it crested the top of one hill and we could see along the roadway straight ahead, I had a very strange experience.

It was like seeing something happen and you know that you dreamed that very scene, and you know what someone will say next or what will be around the next corner. It lasts for just a few seconds really, but it is both wonderful and chilling at the same time. When we drove over the crown of that hill, we could see at least five ridges of hills ahead of us, ahead of where we were going. They were beautiful and lined across the landscape like a painting, one after the other into the eastern distance.

I knew them; it was as if I had already dreamed this moment in the journey, and for reasons I cannot explain, my eyes started to tear up. I blinked the tear away and said to Cully, "There's an old schoolhouse where we turn here. Somebody has made it their home now." We took the fork to the right, and there the old white schoolhouse was, a steep-roofed clapboard box perched in a side-hill meadow, a flower garden red and yellow and orange just outside the front door. Then it passed and the dream memory was over. The road was unfamiliar again, and I could not call back the mysterious recognition.

It was still but mid-afternoon when we started down the last long hill to the Strongs' home; yet that brief time my mind filled itself with strange visions of possibilities and mind-whirling variations on what could happen.

When we finally pulled up before the large white frame house, it was a wonder that I could walk without wavering. Nervousness, doubts, questions, and excitement meshed to create an unsteady heart and mind and body.

Mrs. Strong came to the door when we rapped with the brass knocker, an almost tiny, white-haired woman whose aspect was that of a total stranger to me. Even so, I hesitated when introducing myself, more than half believing that I was now seeing my own mother.

She quickly realized who Cully was and looked him over with much cooing and delight, a grandmother seeing her grandson for the first time, and he already well into his twelfth year.

She said that Anna had gone to the hen house to get the eggs and showed Cully the way to get there, knowing the great joy that would erupt when they met. Cully was off at a run, his quick strides making him look natural and at home as he dashed through the knee-high grasses, like any young boy romping on his grandparents' farm. I followed behind, briskly but trying not to appear too eager nor to arrive so close as to interfere in any way with the meeting of mother and son. My own story would wait a little.

Cully skirted the mill pond and as he neared the small building, a woman turned the corner and started along the path toward him. She was raven-haired, slender, and wore a blue dress with a brown and white apron hung around her neck and snugged at the waist. There was no doubt that she was Anna.

She saw Cully almost at once and just as quickly knew who he was, setting her egg basket down and running to him with her arms wide, sweeping him into her embrace and swinging him back and forth with joyous excitement.

Both were crying as they shared their warm and powerful reunion. They turned, hand-in-hand to start back to the house, and Anna, for the first time, noticed me standing ten yards or so up the path. She was startled, then seemed to remember whatever mention Cully had made of me in his letter, for she composed herself, wiped away tears, and greeted me warmly as I introduced myself.

It was an awkward moment for me, not knowing whether I was a stranger, a possible suitor, or her brother. Well, I was a stranger, no matter which of the other two was accurate, but still it was an odd situation which I decided to treat simply as a visitor to the farm might have. My mind raced with the things I wanted to say, the questions I needed to ask. My emotions swirled like the prairie wind; my words, however, were shaped to be polite and proper, the words of a friend who has escorted a child from a great distance back to his home.

It was soon clear that Mrs. Strong and Anna were the only people still living in the house, a long two-storey built by Mrs. Strong's father-in-law and spacious enough to house a large family in its six bedrooms. Mr. Strong had recently died, just last April they said, but even before that none of the three sons had chosen to stay on the home place. The little family burial plot in a field just west of the house had his grave and, in contrast to the others of earlier times, a white headstone.

My interest was not in the three sons who left but the one who had "disappeared"; yet I waited until the third day to venture into that subject with Anna. In between we worked at straightening the study her father had left in disarray, setting all the books back on the shelves and arranging them by interest. Anna hesitated when she picked up a book about Roman history and slowly flipped through a few pages. Her father had handwritten notes in the margin, I could see, and she was reading those, not the book itself.

I chose to speak with her because I thought it would be less difficult for her to recall this memory than it would have been for Mrs. Strong. I feared that it would be likely to elicit disbelief, rejection, denial from her, and there would then be no way that she could accept me if I were that long-disappeared son. Also, with Anna I might be able to search, find out the weight of probability before asserting that I was he. I did not want to be wrong nor to make a fool of myself before the Strongs. Most of all, I did not wish to bring any pain.

It was easy to fashion a reason for staying, and the luck of having Jeremy Danielson back in Weed to take care of the animals there made my delay a comfortable one. There was so much work that the neglected farm needed done, and the clearing up and setting it right was a wonderful rationalization for me to linger and generate the courage to explore what I really wanted to know.

Cully and I started clearing the yard of brush and limbs, working our way toward the near meadow. Down in an overgrown gully we found two old cars, a black Model T Ford and a large maroon Packard with the word "Super" on the trunk by the lid, and a place where another word had broken off and been lost. Both cars were wide open to the weather and slowly settling into the ground, their tires flat, as the weeds grew up around them. Naturally we both had to sit inside them and get the feel of these relics, their age showing on the rusting spark and throttle levers of the Ford, their seats dry and cracked and somehow comfortable. The dashboard of the Packard was sun-faded and peeling. Cully sat behind the high hard steering wheel and pretended to drive, and I knew we had found the site of many hours of playing for his future days.

I had seen this practice in Ohio and in Illinois: cars no longer deemed useful were, like old horses, set out to pasture. They gradually gathered there, over the years, in a kind of casual order, and seemed as if reminiscing about their better days and the roads they had seen. The worst of places had them jumbled in a haphazard junk heap; the best, in rows or some other orderly arrangement as if left with care and a sense of reluctance in parting with an old friend. These two on the Strongs' place had been parked side by side out of sight, comfortable but not visible from the highway, driven to their resting-place with some planning and concern. They were a pleasure to visit again.

It happened that in the second week there Cully was with Mrs. Strong in the kitchen as Anna went again to feed the chickens and gather the eggs. I walked with her. We had by now become friendly. She told me of applying for a job in a thread mill, but they had not hired her yet so she was giving occasional piano lessons. I had already spoken several times about my life in Illinois, John's passing, my finding Cully, Clara's abandonment of the farm, and Cully's and my life together these last months. It was not unusual, then, that I should say to her as we neared the pond, "Tell me about your family, your brothers, I mean."

She did, speaking a bit of the days when they were young, then describing in detail the different personalities of the brothers and why each had left to start his own life, one in western Connecticut, one in Vermont, the third in Pennsylvania. She did not mention that there had been a fourth.

"And what of your childhood?" she asked. We had now stopped by the pond, and I asked if we might sit on the bank while we talked. The crisp, clear air of late June made the grasses cool and soft, and we sat facing the pond, its smooth surface mirroring the white pines of the hillside on the far bank.

"That's an interesting question," I began, "because there's much about my early childhood that I don't know." In response to her questioning look, I told of the orphan train and being raised by the Andersons.

"But you don't remember anything before that? Nothing?"

"Yes, I do remember some names, names like Willimantic.

"The name Palcher or something like that, but they are very foggy and distant. It was so long ago and my life started again with the Andersons, erasing whatever scant memory there may have been. In fact," and here I hesitated because this would be the first small step, "I am not sure that Gunnar is my actual name. I wish now I still had that white tag that had been attached to my coat when I was on the orphan train. That may have had my name on it. It may have been John. It may have been something else. But the Andersons chose Gunnar and I have become Gunnar fully in the ensuing years. It's a good name, don't you think?" It was a foolish question, a silly question, but it was a momentary deflection and it eased the tension that was building inside me. I did not tell her of my misty recollection of the name Strong.

"But you remembered 'Willimantic'?" she asked. "Does that mean that you were raised there? Do you think that your first family was from around here?"

"It may have been. It seems a strong possibility. That's what I hope to find out."

"How old were you when you went on the orphan train?" she asked.

"Seven, I think. Six or seven." I looked for a spark of reaction in her face. There was none.

"Oh, the poor child. No wonder it is so hard for you to remember." She paused, thinking, interested in the unknown child who I had been, caught by the mystery of my lost childhood. "And from that unusual beginning you have done such wonderful things," she said, "and made such a name for yourself."

"Not really," I said. "I just help people."

We had veered too far from the way I wanted this talk to go, so I decided to open the delicate discussion again, even with heart pounding. "Anna, as Cully and I came east, we took a side trip to Strongsville." It was news which clearly caught her by surprise.

"Oh," she said, a quiet, pensive, even somber sound as she began to understand that I knew more about her past than she had realized, and it was not a past which she herself particularly wanted to recall. "Did Cully tell you about Strongsville?" she asked.

"Indirectly, yes, not much, but he told me enough to make me want to go there and try to start his . . . or our search from that place." I told her about Cully's mention of "their town" and other bits which had led me to link the name Strong with the town of Strongsville. "We even went back to the house where he and you had once lived, but he did not remember it and the people living there knew nothing of earlier owners.

"But what we did do in Strongsville was to read in the records at the town clerk's office and then go to the town library and find a book on the history of the Strong family. You are in it, did you know that?"

"No," she said softly, and I worried now about having probed too deeply into her life and offending her at having done so. Yet it was necessary and I explained as best I could why it was useful to learn about the family. But the important facts still remained unsaid.

"Anna," I began, "In the book, it listed another brother, a boy who it said had disappeared when he was still young."

"Yes," she said, "there was."

She did not continue, and I didn't know whether to ask more questions and risk opening a subject that was obviously painful for the family or let this much rest for now and hope to be able to take it further on another day. My inner anxiety, however, made it clear that the questions would be asked this day or not at all.

"Can you tell me about him?"

"His name was Augustus." She paused again, as if deciding whether she could tell me more. "Father named him that because he had been reading <u>Lives of the Noble Romans</u> and liked the name, thought it had stature and power. I think we ruined that plan by calling him 'Gus.'" She smiled quickly, glanced my way, and then turned back to the pond. A cardinal flew across the pines, mirrored by its twin in the glistening water. She did not continue.

"May I ask you a question about Augustus?"

"Yes."

"The book in Strongsville said that he had 'disappeared' at the age of seven. What does that mean?"

Again she was silent, turning over in her mind, perhaps, the answer she would offer me. Then: "It means that we don't know what happened to him. He did something bad and apparently was so ashamed that he ran away. We never saw him again."

"Ran away?"

"We looked everywhere. Even the river," she gestured toward the east where the stream known as Dimmock's River flowed slowly past, "this pond, the woods, the roads, barns, other towns, stores, neighbors' . . . everywhere. He just disappeared."

"You never heard anything at all?"

"No. Nothing. He was here one day and then he was gone. The search went on for some time and it wore Mother down. She grieved as if Augustus had died, but there was no ending, no burial, no place to know that he was there. Father led the search and spent days and days on it, using all his money and selling our livestock. When Gus was not found and not a single clue had come out, Father simply became silent for many weeks. The rest of his life . . . all these years . . . he was burdened by this guilt of his favorite son whom he had lost.

"Robert and Elan and Matthew finally could not endure this perpetual gloom, and one by one they fled the farm. I did, too. I went with John, my father standing there on the porch dressed in black still and glowering at us as we left. He did not smile. He did not lift his hand in a wave. He did not say 'good luck' or anything. He just looked bereft. It was my escape.

"He had liked John at first, liked having a strong young man at the house, but he hated John in the end for taking me away. He never spoke a word to me after that. When I returned to help mother care for him, he was already dead in spirit, and the following spring he had a stroke and lingered helpless for nearly another year. We never should have left the two of them alone in that house. It was a sad house. We made it even sadder by leaving."

As she told this story, soft tears slid unimpeded down her cheeks, and I knew that the memories had brought images to her mind and she was again seeing and hearing all those sad moments and reliving them. The voices, the gestures, the sounds even of the wheels in the driveway had returned and with them the guilt she felt at having left her parents in an empty house with all their children fleeing, believing that all love had vanished.

We sat without speaking for a very long time. The sky was blue and clear, filled with darting barn swallows, a sky of delight and happiness and promise.

"Shall we gather the eggs?" I asked.

"No. Not yet. It is good that I tell you this. It may help me to at last say it to someone, it has been inside me for so long." She reached over and put her hand over mine as it lay beside me on the grass. "Is that all right?" she asked. "You are a kind listener. Do you mind my telling you all this?"

Her touch was warm and I wanted to take her hand, but I did not. I did not move, and her hand on mine was gentle and carried far more meaning than she ever realized. "Yes," I said. "I want to hear about your life, and then when there is time, I will tell you my story, too."

"John did not succeed and we moved from Ohio to Indiana . . . two places in Ohio . . . and then into Illinois, always looking for the one place where his hard work would be successful. The crops were poor, the prices were low, and we barely crimped by. Cully was old enough to go to school but we lived where there weren't schools, there weren't towns, there weren't people. But we tried and it seemed that we would never succeed. Our lives together hardened.

"Then one day in Illinois a letter came from a neighbor here. She had gotten the address from my note home at Christmas. Mother had left it on the counter for months, she said, and one day she copied it down and wrote to me. She told me that Father was probably failing and that Mother could not possibly cope with him and the empty house and the farm going to ruin. She said she thought Mother was losing her senses, speaking sometimes to empty chairs, setting six places at the table, doing things which showed that she still imagined that the family was intact.

"John said I should stay with him, and the dilemma made my heart heavy. When I decided that I had to go, John told me to stay, and we had a fight . . . another fight. I thought I would be coming back, I thought Cully would spend half the year with me until I could return, I'm not sure what I thought. But I knew that at that moment I had to try to help my father.

"When I got back, father probably had lost his mind, but he was soon unable to move or speak. When he died last April, it seemed to free Mother, and she began to regain life a little. But I could not leave her alone. She is so much better now, and you see the way she treats Cully, so glad to have him here. I think she sometimes believes that Gus has returned, but she still knows who Cully is and the house again has love in it."

In the pause, I noticed that behind us on the state road, a car occasionally passed. A cow bellowed in a distant meadow, and the water's current flowed slowly and quietly to a small dam at the far end of the pond, then spilled with a continuous rush over the dam onto the rocks below. But when Anna spoke, it was as if all other sounds ceased. I heard only her.

The story she told seemed unimaginable: all this heartbreak because a seven-year-old boy had run away? I was not certain that I still wanted to be Augustus Jared Strong any longer. Doc Anderson was a good person, a strong person, his own griefs buried and a full life ahead. Would Gus's return now bring happiness back into this shattered house? I wasn't sure it would.

Yet the answers of the past must be found, of course, for there to be a future.

CHAPTER 34

Cully

It is fun to be here and be with Ma again. We talk and walk, and even Grandma Strong comes with us on some of the walks. We go down a small curvy road and turn off onto a path that goes deep into the woods, and we sit down by a brook and have a picnic sometimes.

Doc and I work in the garden and are getting it into pretty good shape. The season is not so far along here as in Illinois where we lived, so it is not too late to plant many vegetables, even though they may come in a little later than usual. There are some old tools in the garage, and I think he misses his work with the animals back in Weed. He doesn't talk about it, but I think he does.

Doc even gets to talk to a neighbor about his hogs, and he has started up a friendship with the vet here.

A funny thing happens two days ago. Ma asks me, "What would you like to do on your birthday?" I had forgotten that soon it is my birthday. I did not have one last year, and the year before that was just before Pa died. I am surprised when she says it and I guess my smile is big because she seems very happy.

I say, "I would like a big chocolate cake with thirteen candles."

"What else would you like?" she asks.

I think for a while and then remember. I ask Doc and he says okay, so I tell Ma "I would like to go see the circus."

Ma looks surprised, but Doc says, "We saw the posters for one in Hartford when we came through, and I think it is next month. Why don't we all go?" and he looks over at Grandma Strong, but she says "No. You three will go and have a good time. That'll be too far for me. No, no, too much activity for me."

So we talk about it some more and make our plans. Ma and Doc and I will go on a Wednesday because it is a day she does not give any lessons.

We are working on writing, too. We tell Mrs. Strong about our trip, and she says that it is such an interesting story that we must set it down on paper. Doc does not think we need to do that, but she keeps saying "Do it" and pretty soon we begin. We decide to start for me with the day Pa dies and for Doc with the day he first sees me. That way we will get it all down, we think. Then we will put both parts together to make a book. We write for about an hour each morning, and then for a short while after dinner each night.

The writing is easy because it is what we know, and I am surprised at how quickly it goes. Ma comes in one day and asks if she can read what we have so far, but Doc slaps his writing pad closed fast and says that she has to wait until it is finished, so I do the same. No one is going to read it until it is done. Doc says he wants to read it over and improve some parts, but I think he is just bashful. He has never written much before. I have.

We have to write in school no matter where you go, so I am used to it.

Many times I write about sad things, but Doc says that it is all right to do if that is what you remember most. He says the happy times are in the spaces and everyone will know that. So I go ahead and tell it all. It isn't sad to do it here. This is a good place. The meals are good, the bed is big and soft, and I have a huge room of my own with an oak wardrobe in it with a mirror. Doc has his own room, too, only his wardrobe is made of cherry.

We go into the nearest town, Stafford Springs, to buy me some clothes. It is a small town, Ma says, but it looks big to me. It has a railroad track running right along the main street and a black pufferbelly comes through town while we are there and blows his whistle for the crossing so loud that I have to cover my ears. It stops at the Central Vermont depot there, still puffing and puffing even though not moving, and then when it starts up again the engineer lets it have full power and the big iron wheels spin and then start pulling the train slowly away. It has forty-seven cars, coal cars and flat cars and box cars, even three passenger cars, and when the caboose comes by, the conductor on the back waves to me. After it has rounded the bend to follow the river out of town, the smell of the smoke still is in the air. It is a smell I like, an exciting smell.

I notice that Doc is standing next to me now, staring after the train even when we can't see it any more. He says, "It was just like that!" and his face looks as if he has just remembered something as he smiles and looks from me to Ma and then down the tracks again following the train.

My clothes from the trip are getting worn out and some of them are too small now. In that town is what Ma calls a five-and-ten store, and next to that is a clothing store, and they buy me some dungarees and socks with stripes at the top, some new soft shirts, and two pair of shoes, one for good and one for working in the garden and feeding the hens. I'll wear the good ones when we go to the circus for my birthday.

I like being here.

PART VII

Mergings

CHAPTER 35

Doc

We did gather eggs that day. A happy voice calling to us from up the path closed the conversation, as Cully came along to join Anna and me for the rest of the afternoon. That afternoon I watched Cully watching the barn cat. He followed its movements intently for perhaps thirty minutes, then returned to the porch where I was trimming the bushes back.

"Well?" I asked.

"Cats can't glance," he said.

"Can't glance?"

"No. They have to look at something straight on. Dogs can glance out of the side of their eyes or up or down without moving their heads. Cats can't do that. They have to turn their heads and face what they want to see. They'd be even better hunters if they could glance."

"You're right. This farm will be a good school for you."

Two days later as Anna showed me around the farm's remote fields, we returned to the story of thirty years ago. Wild flowers and weeds thrived in the pastures no longer trampled and cropped by cows, sumac had begun to return to the open spaces, and the old trails made by cows wending back to the barn had grown faint.

"Anna," I said, "the other day when you were telling me about Gus, you said that he had done something wrong and had run away."

"Yes. He did."

"What did he do?"

"He accidentally set fire to the barn and almost the house, too. The barn was destroyed."

"What? He was just seven years old."

"I know. That was what made it all so hard to understand. He was trying to help. Father was always very firm that the boys should work to help on the farm, and being seven was no excuse. Matthew was only nine, but he went off with the others that day to cut timber in the wood lot. Gus had to stay here because it might be dangerous work. I was down cellar doing the laundry; Mother was in the kitchen.

"Gus was so sure that he could help, and he felt bad about being left behind. Father was very sharp with him. They had been cutting brush behind the barn and had a big pile of it there. Gus decided he would do that job himself, I guess, and he came into the house and got the box of matches from the shelf by the stove. Mother did not notice him. He probably poured some coal oil on the brush; then he lit it. He must have been terrified almost at once."

Her voice was still as quiet as on the other day, but her eyes were closed as she saw the scene again, and her face responded to the impending tragedy as it was reborn in her words. We sat on a large gray boulder that bulged out of the field, and the sun added its fire to the story I was about to hear.

"I was downstairs and did not know what was happening for quite a while. Then Mother came to the top of the stairs and called down: 'Anna? Are you down there?' 'Yes,' I said. 'Is something burning?' she asked. I looked around and sniffed the air but I saw nothing and all I smelled was the hot soapy water and the bleach. 'No,' I said, 'not down here.' The wood furnace was cold; the large cement basement was dry except where wash water had spilled off into the drain. 'Something's burning,' she said loudly, and I hurried back up the stairs. Together we went out onto the front veranda and off to the right near the barn saw the flames.

"The brush pile was blazing high, sparks flying off with the wind and its heat so strong that the barn behind it seemed to be wavering. We did not see Gus. We did not know then what was really happening; we were just frightened by the size of the brush fire and no one around to tend it.

"We ran out to the fire with the idea of somehow pulling it down . . . getting a rope behind it and pulling from each side to try to spread the brush out on the ground some, there was no water anywhere near by . . . but when we got close we knew that it was far too hot and we saw that the barn had already caught and the side of it was becoming a sheet of flame. It was dry wood and was burning fast.

"Already we knew that there was no way to save the barn. It still had much dry hay inside. All the animals were out except the two horses, and they were nearly mad with fear, neighing and banging inside their stalls. When I opened the stall gate, one horse went quickly into the side pen and I ran him far out into the field. The other seemed crazed, making a sound like a person screaming almost, desperate to escape but blinded by fear and charging into walls. It was too hot for me to stay in the barn any longer, and huge chunks of burning hay were dropping from the loft down into the main floor, starting fires there, too. I ran out too scared to stay inside the barn any longer, knowing we would lose the roan, giving up, but as I cleared the doorway he almost trampled me and bolted through the open door into the clearer air of the side pen and then into the pasture.

"That was when I saw Gus. He was standing near the old catalpa tree at the driveway fork, standing but hunched over, his hands curled up in front of his chest as if he were cold, and he was crying and looking at the fire and at me and saying, 'I didn't meant to do it. I didn't mean to do it' in a shrieking, hysterical cry. I said, 'Stop crying and come on and help! We need you!' but he did not move.

"I knew he was safe there, at least, and I had got the horse out and off into the field. When I got back to the side where the fire started, Mother stood weeping with her hands covering her mouth as she watched the fire. The whole roof and another side were now blazing.

"In the woods, Father and the boys saw the smoke rising out of the valley, and they drove the truck back down from the wood lot. They tried to get a hose hooked up to the house, but it was too late to save the barn. The roof dropped in and the big beams poked up through. One fell sideways almost to where Elan was standing, a sound that was like a tree falling during a storm.

"Father got the boys to spray water on the house so that the heat and sparks would not start that burning if the wind should shift, but the barn was gone. It was entirely burned, even still glowing into that dark night. When we finally stopped fighting the fire and knew the house was safe, we realized that Gus was not there. At first, Father was afraid that he had been in the barn, but I told them I had seen him by the tree and that he was scared and hiding somewhere, knowing the thrashing he would get. But we did not find him even though we called and called all night.

"In the morning, the jagged black timbers that had not burned up sent curling trails of bitter smoke into the red, red sunrise." Her closed eyes squeezed even tighter together. "It was an ugly ruin. The air was terrible with the smell. And Gus was gone. All we found was the box of stove matches by the tree. He must have dropped them there."

She leaned far forward, her forehead just touching her knees, her hands folded at her waist and hidden now in her leaning. She seemed to be staring at the rock between her feet, a rough gray patched with curled white scale of various shades, its pocked surface home to stray seeds and an occasional wandering ant.

There was no where to go now. My searching journey had ended abruptly, consumed in the now dead thirty-year-old flames of an accidental fire, transformed into sooty vapor by a well-meant act of a very young boy. The conversation was not over, but I was convinced that my hope of solving the riddle of my youth was gone. Gus had disappeared again and, in a sense, so had I.

If anything would have lived in Gus's memory, even if he had been transported to some far inland state and raised by another family, it would have been that fire. I had absolutely no recollection of such a conflagration in my past.

"You mentioned Mrs. Strong's sometimes thinking Cully might be Gus," I said at last when her hand moved back and forth over the stone, as if smoothing the thousands of years in its scarred surface. "Have people always believed that Gus would return?"

"No. No. They did not believe that. Just the opposite," she said, brushing her hair back slowly with her hand and looking up into the sun.

"I'll show you when we go back to the house."

It was both a pain and a lifting to know that I was not Gus, that the similarities which had led me into this fanciful and even exciting possibility were merely coincidences, chance mergings of details which might have happened a thousand times to a thousand people and which meant nothing. Nothing at all. The Strongs did not expect Gus to return, and he hadn't.

We slid down off the boulder, brushed off the grains of stone that clung to our clothes, and Anna smoothed away her tears, brushing them with both hands outward across her cheeks. We walked back along our own trail of trodden grasses toward the house.

She led me toward the small family graveyard out away from the house. "Here," she said, "is Father's grave," standing in front of the white stone marked only with the name "Harlan." She pointed to another, a small stone nearly flat with the earth, and when we moved over to it I saw that it said "Augustus Jared Strong" and the dates on it were his birth date and the date of the fire. He had, for them, died the day he disappeared.

"No," she said again, exactly as she had said it in the field, "No. We did not expect that he would ever come home."

When we arrived back at the house, the smells of baking enriched the air and drove away the last spare thoughts of the smoldering barn. Squash pie and sugar cookies, made with Cully's help and, undoubtedly, his expert tasting skills, now rested in the pantry, the pie cooling and the cookies wrapped in wax paper and safely stored in a metal box. "These," Cully said, pointing to the cookie box, "we can take with us to the circus."

"That's right," I remembered. "Your big day is coming soon." And I knew that somewhere tucked out of sight there would be a chocolate cake.

That night I suffered a terrible nightmare about a burning barn and a frightened boy running away. It was Anna's story, I knew, come into vivid life in the night, its detail haunting and sharp, chilling me with fear. Yet when I abruptly woke, I was perspiring and lost, not recognizing where I was for several minutes, afraid to move in the silent darkness that seemed a bottomless black chasm around my bed.

Only when I forced myself to sit up on the edge of the bed and my feet touched the wide, cool boards of the floor was I confident of life again.

I told Anna about my dream in the morning, and she felt so sorry that she had caused me such distress.

Thirty Years Earlier . . . III

The Fire

The sharp slap across the face had knocked him sideways onto his arm and hip, scraping them on the gravel driveway.

"I mean it!" shouted his father, the voice seeming to thunder reverberations off the house and barn. "You stay here!" and he climbed in without looking back again and the truck started off, one brother turned and peering out the cab window and the other two, riding on the flat bed, watching him.

He knew the work in the north wood lot was hard and possibly dangerous, that they hated to have him around because they had to watch out for him and he slowed their work. But he was big, even though only six, and he could help.

Then he knew what to do to show them that he should be included . . .

But now it was a swirling night filled with tears and shivering, a cold roadside whose spindly black branches snatched cruelly at him and made shapes behind each tree. The gravel scuffed and pebbles sprayed ahead of him, bouncing and rolling to a still place as he hurried by. Moon-made shapes loomed on both sides, and he knew the road only by looking up and seeing the break in the overhanging trees, following this river of lighter air as if knowing where it led, as if it led anywhere he knew.

Somewhere behind, the orange and inescapable fire diminished, and after twice turning to look back and seeing its frightening sunset glare through the meadow's trees, he did not turn any more and just went on, small steps after small steps, brown shoes making little mark, little sound on the hard road of fear. It had been hours ago, choking breaths uncounted hours ago, running in desperate flight from that certain and thunderous blame, that voice, that destruction now irreversible and life-ending, severing warmth and words and food and bedtime, leaving forever (he knew even at almost seven years) because there could be no explaining, no forgiveness, no life after the stained and sooty skeleton barn still smoldering in the field beyond his mind.

At first, when his match had begun a lifting wall of flames well beyond intent, he had frozen in the face of the flames, rigid and shaking, rooted as if tied like a sacrifice to be engulfed, staring with a tight-throated terror as the fire rose and crackled through the black dry brush and easily reached across to the gray barn, licking the rough side boards in teasing sensuality, then sticking, adhering, becoming one with the boards and sending forth the first low sounds of the roar that was to ice his blood and scorch his arms when he tried to pull a branch from the pile.

It threw him back, heated beyond belief on one side and frozen on the other, bending his small face away from scorching, hotter than any summer hayfield sun, hearing its eerie ghost-like singing in the sap-weeping boards as they spat and turned to black within the flame.

He swirled away as if dizzy, moving under the catalpa tree as he would in a rain, protected by the coolness of its overhanging green against the surging fiery monster which had, in fact, already forgotten him. His running sister shouted to him but he could not hear. He saw her let the roan out of the side yard and turn it loose in the main field, but he did not remember it. He heard her call again, but he did not remember why or what he was to do.

She then was gone, and the snarling flames reached toward him once again, trying to clutch his arms and draw him toward the life-ending heat. He shrank back, bent almost double, hurting in some deep inner part not known before, clutching himself to keep from flying into a thousand pieces and to hold in that awful scream he heard building in his chest. He shrank back across the driveway, across the yard, out of the dragon's grasp and beyond reach of its heat. But still he saw it, higher and more fierce, more angry, blazing above the tree top now, its roar full throated and demonic, viciously circling in the whirlwind air above the flames, searching for him. Shrank back into the gray corner of the storehouse doorway, now a hundred yards from the fire, and shrank to the cold stone steps in hopeless anguish.

He saw the farm truck arrive then, saw others dashing to the flames, saw them moving, stick figures gesturing rapidly and silently as if acting on commands from the ogre he had raised, and he turned and ran, a desperate, breath-panting, stumbling run of tears and fright and total loss. He did not stop nor know where he ran. It was simply terror's need.

CHAPTER 36

Cully

Most of the days are clear and fine, and we write and work the garden, tend the chickens and start to clear the pastures again one at a time.

After work we sit on the veranda and Mrs. Strong tells stories about the old days when the farm was bigger and Ma's brothers were all here and helped. She sits and rocks, but when she gets to an important part, she stops rocking and sits straight.

Lots of times the story has something funny in it, like the time the littlest brother named Matthew was out on the veranda with them, and Mr. Strong went and got his revolver and brought it out. He handed it to Matthew who could hardly hold it because it was so heavy, and he told Matthew to aim it at the chickens that were in the yard and pull the trigger.

Matthew took the gun in both hands, she said, and was very afraid to shoot the chickens, but Mr. Strong told him to go ahead, that he had to do it. Matthew held it tightly and squeezed the trigger as hard as he could, trying to obey his father, but he wasn't strong enough to pull the trigger and make the gun fire. He tried and tried, with the other boys cheering for him and giving him advice, but he couldn't do it and Mr. Strong pretended to be mad.

Elan took the gun finally and pulled the trigger hard and the gun went off with such a loud noise that everybody jumped a little and the chickens leaped up into the air with squawks and wild flapping of wings, and when they came back down started running for about thirty feet. Then they slowed and started pecking the ground again. Then Mr. Strong had a laugh, too, because he had put blanks in the revolver and knew that no chickens would be hurt.

Mrs. Strong is laughing when she tells this story, and she is nearly crying when she says that it was two months before any chicken would come near the house again.

I like her stories. We all do.

One late afternoon after supper . . . they always eat promptly at 4:30 . . . we are sitting on the veranda when a storm comes up. It is a powerful thunderstorm with lots of lightning and wind and loud thunder that makes the house's windows rattle and the maple trees across the yard sway and crack with bending. Once in a while a small limb breaks off and falls to the ground.

We sit there and are safe and dry, but just out ahead of us not more than eight feet is a downpour like a flood coming off the porch roof, and the lightning flashes so bright we all go "Aahhh" when we see it. Sometimes the lightning and thunder come right together, so bright and loud that it is almost more than my eyes and ears can stand. Each time that that happens, somebody says, "That was a close one!" The air smells odd then for a minute, just as if a train has passed, and we all wait eagerly for the next blast.

Doc says that you can tell how far away the lightning is by counting slowly after the flash, and if you get to five, the lightning was a mile away. If you can count to ten, he says, it's two miles away. But if you can feel the hair rise on your arms, the lightning will be very close.

I think my way is just as good. If you hear the thunder with the lightning, it is so loud and is right on top of you, but if you can see the lightning across the valley before the thunder rolls, then it was further away.

These storms seem to come after the hot days more often than not, and we enjoy every one of them Occasionally, somebody's shed or a tree gets hit, but most of the time there is no damage.

I do notice one thing, though. When a storm hits, cows will stay out in the pasture and keep on eating if the farmer has not chased them in. Cows don't seem to hear the noise, see the lightning, or mind getting wet.

But chickens know better. When a storm comes up, you never see any chickens in the yard. They have all gone inside their coop and will stay dry.

Ma asks me about the storms in Illinois, and she seems to think that I understand a lot about farm life. "Doc must have been a good teacher," she says, and he makes me tell her all I have learned about farrier's tools and liniments and treating sick or hurt animals.

She says, "I'm very impressed. I bet I know what you're going to be when you grow up," and she means a veterinarian like Doc and I would like that and grin. We all do.

Just before we go back inside, Mrs. Strong says she has a surprise for me and makes me choose which hand is holding it behind her back. I guess the left one and I am right. It is a box of animal crackers. The box is decorated like a circus wagon, with red and blue and yellow. The crackers are shaped like circus animals.

CHAPTER 37

Doc

"You can't give up on that," Anna had said. "You've got to try to find out."

I knew she was right, but I had changed, I told myself; now finding out who I was had become merely a curiosity, not something vital. Having solved one part of the riddle, I was content to let the other part sleep. It was not important any longer. I was Gunnar Anderson.

I thought that, believed it, and even so knew that it was hollow reasoning. I would keep looking anyway. This was, as Anna sensed, one of those searches that cannot stop just on a whim, a sudden decision, a feeling. If it were to stop at all, it must be because of evidence or a completely cold trail. This trail was surely cool, but even that was enough heat to mean it must continue.

Two days later we were on the road south to Willimantic, prepared to search the records and try to find some clue that would lead to another that would lead to the answer. To get there, we drove past Storrs Agricultural College and I was suddenly nostalgic, remembering my own college days in training for my veterinary degree. We took a side trip through the farm part of the campus, the hog pens, the chicken farm, the horse barns and cattle pastures.

The long sheds of the chicken farm seemed so familiar, and we stopped and got out to walk. The grain smells immediately captured me, and I remembered one day in particular from my student days, back when I liked to write poetry. It was on the college's research farm just outside Columbus. It was a memory that enveloped me and it was a pleasure to live it again as I told Anna.

"Hurry and get the feeding done," Harry had called to me as he walked fast off toward the range chickens. Gray clouds massed toward the southwest. Rain coming.

I did not need to be told. I might do my tasks slowly, but I knew what they were. I entered the middle doorway of the long building known as "B" and walked the concrete aisle to the end. I'd done half the feeding earlier and could finish the row in ten minutes, maybe fifteen. I already had an idea for what to do during the rain.

I entered each pen and cleaned the water dish, filled the tray with stone bits for the hens to peck, and made sure the self-feeding towers were full. As I walked through the pens, the chickens hardly noticed me, yet they maneuvered skillfully so as not to be in the way, sometimes hustling with a squawk and quick steps if they felt imperiled.

In pen 7 the broody hen was back in the nest again, and I reached in and lifted her out, getting a few quick pecks on the back of my hand. The birds were testy when they were broody; my hand and arm showed that. But I'd pull them out and raise the trap door again, knowing that in a few minutes the broody one would hop back in the nest, trigger the trap door into falling, and again be caught there until I came by to let her out. Nothing smart about them when they were broody.

After the feeding was finished, I looked up at the towering dark sky and felt the slight wind shift, left B and went to the feed shed, knowing no one else would be in there during the rain; they all went into the battered old office where there was a torn, slumping couch and some scarred wooden chairs where they played high-low-jack for a nickel a point.

I watched the rain come across the slight valley, changing the color from yellow land to gray, almost silvery as the grasses slanted ahead of the breeze and bent under the rain. Slowly it approached, soundless, moving steadily as if it were painting the land, pattering across the dirt yard in small explosions of dust that sank and became merely wet earth. Then it reached the shed, dripping slowly from the chicken-wire window, spattering on the roof in steady, unceasing drum roll, and moving on across into the next yard behind me.

With it came a fresh scent, the scent of life and earth, of wet pure air and spring blueness. It was a smell which always made me feel good, even smile, and its mist touched my face delicately with welcome coolness. I moved close to the window and felt the soft rain on my tongue.

I went to the white wooden shelf where I kept a notebook and pen, climbed up among the grain sacks, found a comfortable position, and from my dry, grain-smelling bed watched the rain fall. The storm had looked gigantic as it came across the fields. There had even been a flash of lightning—probably what had worried Harry—and surely it had seemed that an awesome power was about to wash over us all like a cosmic tidal wave. Instead, it was a soft rain, crisp as only such rains can be to the touch and smell, not soundless yet not pounding either, a rain that farmers pray for and running children love.

The words formed in my mind, a plan, a poem.

Footsteps just outside made me hide the sheets quickly, embarrassed to have chicken farm workers find me writing poetry. They were cursers, physical men of hard hands and black metal lunch pails, of evening radio lives and opaque days; loud men of sharp tongues and caustic arrows for mocking words. The footsteps continued past and faded.

Far off to the right I saw the steam rising off the tar road. Water rising again. To rain again and rise again. The notebook.

The trailing clouds drifted their shadows across the valley now, leaving light behind. I loved to watch the patterns of the clouds, the shifting shapes so recognizable and yet difficult to point out. I had tried with Mrs. Anderson, yet when she looked, the shape had tumbled into another shape and she did not see what I meant. I set my notebook, unopened this time, back on its shelf, the pen caught in between pages, and went out into the cool dampness of the after-rain.

A black car, a Buick, turned noiselessly into the driveway and on large white-walled tires rolled toward me, moving with care and hardly disturbing the puddles it passed through with hisses. It stopped. A man in a jacket and tie stepped half-way out of the open driver's door and asked, "May we look around?"

"Yes, of course," remembering the admonition I had received about this research farm being "for the people" and "paid for by taxes," a small lecture spoken on the day I was assigned this job. The man in the tie and jacket went to the other side of the dark car still shining from the rain, its windows gleaming reflections of the sky and trees.

The man and a dark-haired woman in glasses who seemed to be his wife, led a little girl by the hands, and there was an older woman. Grandma, I thought. The four came to where I was standing by B building and asked about the farm and the range chickens which they could see in the distance now reemerging from their pastel yellow coops.

I spoke of the chickens, how many, and the egg contests and the wing bands with numbers, and the penciled recording of the number on each egg. Then I thought of the obvious: "Come inside the building. Let me show you." I led the way but stopped at the doorway of B and held my arm and hand out to indicate that they were to go in first.

The chickens clucked and walked their pens, one or two glancing at the people out in the aisle. Again I explained about the wing tags, and one large hen hopped up on the roost, flapped her wings, and settled back.

"See," I said. "Just like that. See how big she is?" and for the first time I actually looked at the little girl, knowing that the visit really was for her. Her dress was lovely, white and clean, almost as if she had come to church. Her black patent leather shoes gleamed on the concrete floor, with bright white socks rising high up toward her knees. I pointed for her and then felt very awkward.

She could not see the hen. She was blind. She was hearing sounds but seeing nothing.

I felt foolish, stupid, and suddenly no words came to describe fully what they were seeing. I slipped the latch of the pen and went inside, reaching under and lifting the large hen off the roost with hardly a flutter of wings, cradling the bird with my left arm and stroking her with my right hand.

I carried the surprisingly calm hen out into the aisle and kneeled down before the little girl. "Here," I said, "touch this chicken with your hand. It's all right. You can pet her." I hoped that the chicken thought so, too.

Tentatively the child reached out. The adults watched fixedly, almost smiling, almost fearful that the bird would move suddenly, largely, and scare the small girl. Her finger tips touched the back feathers and she moved her hand along them smoothly. Then her full hand spread onto the hen's back and she smiled as she felt the satin feathers, touching them almost as if she could feel the iridescent colors through her finger tips.

"There," I said, "Isn't she soft?"

"Yes," she said quietly, enthralled, understanding "hen" as never before.

She moved her arms around the bird then, gathering its size and bulk, holding it like a big stuffed animal even though it was still in my arms, too. She seemed startled at first at the legs and feet, sensing them again and again with her fingers, the rough, hard stalks protruding from the warm softness of the body, ending in sharp, callused points.

"The legs are yellow," I said, not knowing if the child knew colors somehow, maybe before she went blind. I didn't know. I glanced at the adults but there was no hint that I had said the wrong thing.

Then she moved her hands against the lie of the feathers, up toward the neck, and I grew nervous, sure that at some point the hen would peck at the unfamiliar touches. I cooed softly to the hen whose eyes looked quite wary. "There, there. It's okay." And the little girl touched the head which jerked out of the way; touched the comb (jerk); felt the beak which astonishingly stayed still long enough for her to understand "beak," as I spoke each time and named the part of the hen she was touching.

Now the big gamble. "Would you like to hold her?" Big smile. She nodded.

Slowly I transferred the hen into the girl's arms, soothing the bird and calming it with steady strokes along its back as the child held it close to her neck and could feel its weight, me keeping a hand underneath just in case.

Then the girl laid her face against the hen's back, her cheek soft against the soft feathers. The hen remained still.

"Thank you so much," said the mother, the first words she had spoken. "Thank you." I saw that she was wiping her cheeks with a hankie, and Grandma had a broad smile on her face, too.

"That's fine," said I. "Very happy to do it. You picked a good time. Isn't this a beautiful afternoon?"

"Yes," said the father. "It's turned out to be quite a nice day." They began to get back into their car. I went back to the notebook, quickly, for the rest would be resuming their work.

> *Drops of rain*
> *Each time they tumble*
> *From heaven-shrouding clouds*
> *Are very self-assured.*
>
> *Theirs is an endless life,*
> *For each knows that soon*
> *It will rise again into*
> *The kingdom of God.*

The car doors had shut with four unmistakable thumps. The Buick motor started. The sound of turning, of leaving. I realized then, too late, that I did not know the little girl's name and this was a poem for her.

I smiled at Anna in the silence of the story's end.

I looked at her, embarrassed at having been so carried away into the remembrance. "You can do that here, too, you know," Anna said, her eyes moist and lighted with a clear and luminous sparkle that spoke more than words. "Dr. Phelps is getting on and needs a good person to work with him. He likes you. Why don't you have that talk with him?"

Her optimism and faith that had survived the dry and barren farm years ignited in me the desire and confidence to start a new life here, lightening for the first time my sense of guilt at having left a land I loved and people I liked. One can do wonders when someone else cares, I learned, a lesson sunk deep in a buried past and now resurfaced to answer even such a simple and basic question as "What am I doing here?" This might be the answer. I'd consider going to discuss a job with Dr. Phelps. If he agreed, I would write to Jeremy Danielson and have my equipment shipped by rail to the depot we had passed.

"Perhaps I will," I said.

When we reached the city clerk's office in Willimantic, we faced another puzzle. Where to start looking? I told the clerk, a woman named Clara Devaney, what we were trying to find, and she took great interest in the search.

"How old are you?" she asked. "We can start with the records from that year."

I answered. "Thirty-six, maybe thirty-seven, I am not exactly sure."

"Good," she said. "Then we will look back at the birth records for those years and see whether something strikes a chord." She went into a back room and brought forth two volumes of records, set them on a table, brought over another chair for Anna, and we began the search. Mrs. Devaney joined us.

Nothing. Many boys had been born that year, some with unusual given names. Augustus Strong was there, but nothing brought any hint to my mind that any of them might be my name. Neither first nor last names seemed personally familiar.

"Then let's try this," she said. While we had been looking at the birth records, she had brought out a green book which bulged with newspaper clippings set into pages beside names and dates. These were all the deaths that occurred six and seven years after the births in the books just studied. After each name was the age of the person at death. Sometimes the exact date of the death was listed. Many times the cause of death was given, as well.

"Sometimes," Mrs. Devaney said, "families record lost and vanished people as 'dead' if they have abandoned all hope of ever finding them. It's possible your family might have done that in this case." Anna gave me a look, obviously remembering how the Strongs had treated Gus's disappearance when they had given up hope.

Some of the notations were brief stories of their own, sad hints of domestic tragedy which, in raising our sympathies, nearly distracted us from our own search. One read: "James Mallon, 8, killed by the cars." Another: "William Brimley, 14, drowned while swimming with his dog in Bolton Pond." A third: "Charles Rutherford, 42, found hanged from tree in woods across from Layton residence, Route 32."

There were children listed there, boys aged six or seven. Small pox, accidents, diphtheria, scarlet fever, one from a beating, horse trampling, one listed simply as "machinery." None who disappeared, none stolen away, none kidnapped. One "wandered away and got lost in the woods," but he was younger, only four.

"What else can we try?" I asked. We had already been looking for more than two hours.

"Well, you could try the 'Chronicle" office and see what they have, but I doubt that you'll find anything there that's not in these records. Looking through newspapers that are thirty-some years old is a very tedious process."

She paused, pursed her lips, and made a small show of thinking. Clara Devaney was obviously enjoying this unusual challenge. "Let me think, where could we look to find out what happened to someone whose name we don't know?"

She said it quietly, musing to herself as she thought, but the actual statement made the search sound so preposterous that I laughed out loud. She went right on.

"Your hope is that you'll see a name and it will ring a bell? Right?"

I nodded, "Yes."

"You might just try a systematic walk through the cemeteries, but, no, you'd have to look in so many. Walk up and down the rows and all. Some of the stones are just about impossible to read, of course those are ones much older than you're looking for. They're from the 1700's mostly. There's the Catholic one on Broad Street, and the Baptist one over off Carver Street, the Methodist one and the Congregationalist one behind the church and the Jewish one and the Reformed one and a couple others. And that would still miss all the small private ones some families have on their own land. And then there's the likelihood that there's no grave at all, seeing as there wasn't a body. Lordy, lordy, how are you going to find out?" Another long pause while Anna and I waited, somewhat impatiently now, I have to admit. "I can't say as I know! You don't know which neighborhood to ask around in. You don't know where the father might have worked. Are you even sure Willimantic is the right place to look?"

"No, I'm not sure of anything. The only thing I'm becoming sure of now is that it wasn't Willimantic."

"Well, that may be true. You don't recall any name, any other name that might help?"

"I do seem to remember the name Palcher," I said, "but we haven't seen that here anywhere."

Mrs. Devaney thought about that for a while. "No," she said, "I know just about every family name and there's no Palcher in Willimantic." She named a few which were similar, she thought, Pitcher, Pickard, Palmer, Palmerston, Patterson, Belcher. No, none of those.

"I don't know where that name Palcher comes from," I said. "I think maybe it was the name of a woman who went with us on the train. I don't know what else it could be. She was with us just for a few days and that was all. Somehow the name stuck. Probably wasn't someone here at all."

We thanked Mrs. Devaney, left her our telephone number just in case, and went out to the car, remarking on the experience of meeting someone like her. It had led nowhere yet had been somewhat enjoyable, but the key fact was that Anna and I had done it together and, I believed, had grown closer in this common effort.

"What will we try next?" asked Anna.

"We'll try the same thing in each neighboring town, I guess, until all the possibilities within reason have been used up and we either have found the answer or realize that there isn't one. We can't do this forever. Can we try one a day or one every other day? How many are there?"

Anna paused for a moment, counting them off on her fingers while she thought. "Without going too far off there would be six" and she named them, all towns surrounding Willimantic.

And so we began, eliminating them one by one with increasing efficiency. At the end of the six, we tried two more which were closer to the Strongs' house than to Willimantic and had the same result. If I had lived there and left there, no record of it existed.

I wrote to the New England Children's Aid Society in both Boston and Hartford, hoping, but found that the letters quickly came back unopened. The offices had closed, the project was over, no forwarding address. A search turned up the name of a person who had been an officer in the organization, but she said the records had been lost or destroyed or put in a vault somewhere; in short, she had no knowledge now, so many years later, of what had occurred thirty years ago. She gave me other names.

"That was just about the last year," she said. "The NECAS was nearly shut down by then and it did close a year later. I doubt those records have been saved anywhere."

I disagreed, although I did not say that to her. I thought that they probably had. Someone keeps such things in boxes in an attic or cellar, a spare room or a warehouse for years and years until someone else finds them many decades later and decides they are not worth anything and throws them out, throwing out history with them. Personal history. Throwing out lives. But no one I could find had any idea whether such records still existed.

Everyone I spoke with was quite helpful and generally seemed to remember their work in a totally positive light, finding good homes by placing out orphans and helping Christian people who wanted children in the Midwest. No, they all said, they never simply took children just to fill quotas. "No," they said, "that was unthinkable."

"Why not try . . ." they'd say, helping, giving me the name of someone else to contact.

And I did contact them, contacted them all, many calls a day for several days. "Call Jim Southern," one man had said, "he'd know if anyone would. He'll know for sure." Jim Southern had died two years earlier. That path, too, had ended.

One afternoon Anna and I were driving westward toward Tolland and had come down the long hill that leads to the West Ashton rail station and the river when we saw a stopped passenger train in the valley at the depot. Smoke lifted from the stack in gentle, unhurried streams, not the churning coal-smelling clouds of power. "Come on," I said, "I've got to see something."

We reached the station yard and turned in, gently bouncing over the dirt parking area with its large undulating bumps, and parked beside the gray station with its black and white sign: ASHTON. The dark green train bound for New London sat there. "We're waiting for some mail to be loaded," the conductor said. I asked and he said we could step aboard for a couple minutes. "Of course," he said, glancing up the tracks toward the engine as if looking to see if anyone was watching. "We won't pull out for fifteen minutes or so. I'll give you plenty of warning," he said.

So Anna and I climbed the three black-steel steps onto the platform and turned left through the narrow door into the empty passenger car. The western sun slanted in and illuminated the mote-filled air like beams in a religious painting.

We stood there silently for a soundless minute, peering through the beams along the rows of maroon seats toward the other end of the car, and I was moved through time. "Smell that?" I exclaimed to Anna. "It's the same! It's just like the orphan train! It's that same musty, dry smell of the seats!" I stepped forward down the aisle and, touching the back of one of the seats, ran my hand over the fabric, again. The feel was thirty years old and yet fresh in my mind and fingertips.

I hadn't remembered that until now, but the train in Stafford had made me think I just might if I climbed into a railroad car again. And it was true: the smell of that car and the touch of the seats had transported me back into a memory I had completely forgotten, and I knew exactly what the train's motion would feel like if it started. I sat down and rubbed my hand back and forth over the seat, sensing its age and its stories. I looked up at Anna and tears filled my eyes.

For a moment the train moved into darkness, swaying in a clacking rhythm over the rails, an occasional light flashing past my window, and a child sobbed. Another young voice called out harshly, "Shut up an' go ta sleep!" It startled me and jarred me back.

Anna sat across the aisle, silent. I leaned out into the aisle to see down the rows of seats to the far door, then sat back again and closed my eyes so I could remember as much as possible. It was difficult to hold the images in my mind for long. They would appear and then flit away and, often, would not come back until I could sense the air and the texture just right. Then they would fade again.

I looked out the window. The train's shadow stretched away over the ground and track bed of the north-bound line. Its dark unmoving silhouette outlined the windows, darkened a section five feet up a telegraph pole, then continued onto the ground again.

The door abruptly snapped open at the forward end of the car.

"We're about ready to pull out!" called the conductor.

"Thanks," I said, a muffled word, and I waved my hand to show I had heard.

"Thank you," Anna said as we passed him, moving back onto the hard metal platform and then down the steps onto the ground again, releasing the cold iron handrail, releasing this memory regained at last. He stood on the first step and swung his arm up and down to signal the engineer.

"Are these old cars?" I asked him before the train moved.

"Yes, some of them are pretty old, cars from other lines, kind of semi-retired now on this line. But they're stout and sturdy and will go for a hundred years." The train began its slow roll forward.

I walked along the ties, gradually increasing my pace, keeping up. "You wouldn't know what line these were on?" I asked.

"No, not unless we scraped off some of the side paint and could see what it says underneath," he said, getting louder. "Most of these cars were probably New York Central once, maybe Pennsy. They get replaced there and the CV buys them at low cost and gets them in good shape and off they go." He called loudly now, moving faster, "Yeah, probably New York Central, most of them."

The pace was too rapid for me now. I stopped and he seemed to accelerate, leaning back out from the top step waving to us, growing smaller. We waved back.

I smiled and Anna knew why. It was like rediscovering a lost toy, and it was all the better because she was there to share it and understand it.

Now I was satisfied, willing to allow the search to end. The trail toward a vanished name had led only as far back as some empty town records and forgotten files, but now I had the scent of an old railroad car that would stay forever. I had reached the conclusion I believed was coming, but I had reached it carefully, thoroughly, finally. This part of the journey was over.

The question now was whether to return to Weed. Cully and I discussed it. In Weed, he had said I should stay, that the farmers would need me. Now he did not want me to leave Ashton. This time he was more persuasive. Mrs. Strong said that I could use her late husband's study as my office to get my practice started, perhaps remodel the old garage for a treatment area. Thanks to the kindness of Dr. Phelps, we have begun to plan that already.

Cully found his mother and seems happier than any time I have been with him. Apparently I cannot find out who I was, but I like who I am and want to remain who I have become. Cully will be going to school in the fall, and I can board with the Strongs and help them on their small farm even as I develop my practice.

And there is Anna.

CHAPTER 38

Cully

This is the last chapter I will ever write. I do not want to write this one, but Grandma Strong says I must. Ma says I should, too, so that the whole story will be told. I know I will have to stop many times, but she says maybe if I write it a little at a time, I can do it.

Some things happen and you can't explain why.

Wednesday is my birthday and we go to Hartford to see the circus. It is the Crandall Brothers Circus and is the biggest one in the country, I think.

Getting there takes us back past the jail with the man looking out and the courthouse and we even swing back and forth across the railroad tracks just before Hartford. It is July. We see no train this time, so we drive straight through without having to slow down very much. Doc remembers all these parts of the trip and he points them out to Ma. She says she is amazed at what we have done. Grandmother Strong does not come with us because she says she will get too tired on such a long trip, but she says she will have supper ready for us when we get back. I know that that means birthday cake.

We get to the field where the circus is, with three tents, two small ones and one huge one, and lots of cages still on truck beds, and right away I can smell the animals. It is a good smell, like the smell of the earth, and the sounds of people walking in the straw remind me of the barn in Weed. Lots of the animals are outside where we can see them. It is exciting to stand next to the elephants, so big and gray that they make a shadow over all of us, and their trunks come around and bump our arms and sides and poke into our pockets to search for snacks. We buy peanuts to feed them and they take them into their long gray trunks. Then they curl the trunk under and snuffle the peanuts into their mouths. It's funny how such a big animal likes such a small treat. Their skin does not look like the skin in pictures of them in our school books. It is rough and has bristles in the crossed lines that make millions of wrinkles, not like a cow's side or a horse's. There is one elephant with a box on its back, and we take a ride around the area on him. It's like being up on a moving bridge and the people we pass all stop and look up at us and wave.

There are some camels that look like worn-out rugs, lions and tigers still in their lined-up cages and pacing, zebras that a man has trained to walk around side by side, and some horses with gold and green ribbons in their manes and tails. Farther back are wire dog kennels with the little poodles and other performing dogs waiting for the show to start, just like us.

One man has trained birds, doves and parrots, that walk along his arms and over his head when he tells them to, and one looks at me and says "Hello" so I answer it. These are birds that are comfortable with being trained and owned. I don't see any owls here, and I want to tell him about the owl we saw, but he isn't interested.

It is a warm day but the wind pushes the flags out on top of the tents, and we walk around and look at the animals a long time before Doc buys the tickets and we go inside the biggest tent there. It has very tall red, white, and blue poles holding the top up in four places, and between the bottoms of the poles are wide rings made of curved wooden blocks. Later the animals and clowns do their acts inside these rings.

A man sells us all some pink cotton candy, and Doc buys a souvenir program so we can talk about the circus and show Grandma Strong when we get home. Our seats are on the side, just about half way up, right across from the center ring, and Ma tells Doc that they are very good seats and he says, "Nothing but the best" and is very happy.

In the beginning there is an announcement and the band plays and all the animals and acrobats and clowns go around the edge of the rings in a big parade. It is exciting and fun. There is a huge crowd this afternoon, the whole tent is full, and they cheer and clap and are enjoying the circus just like us. The band music is loud and sharp, very exciting, and the air smells of dirt and straw and peanuts and animals. Doc says there are thousands of people there, more than I have ever seen in one place before. More even than in the whole town of Weed, although those people never get together at once.

After the parade, every ring has some acts in it. Sometimes they will all be horses, sometimes they are all little dogs that do fast tricks and make us laugh. Once they use only the center ring and have seals that balance balls and catch things and play a tune on some pipes so the man will toss them a fish. In between, while one group of animals is leaving and the next is coming in, the clowns race around on one-wheel bicycles or little cars and play tricks on each other. They even pretend to get mad and come over to the audience and throw a pail of water at each other and miss so it goes on the audience, but it is little bits of red, blue, green, and yellow paper, not water at all, and everybody laughs. All the time the announcer in the red coat is telling us how dangerous each act is, especially the ones with the acrobats.

This is the hard part. I don't want to tell it.

It happens when there are tigers in the center ring and the workmen have put up a big cage around the whole ring, and a blond-haired man in a golden suit is inside with the tigers and makes them behave by holding a stool and snapping his long, black whip and shouting commands at them. In the side rings, there are horses with green and yellow plumes on their heads trotting around in a circle while a woman stands on their backs. They seem used to the tigers and are not bothered by the roaring.

A man down on the dirt ground yells something out loud that at first we do not understand, but the band suddenly starts playing a march very loudly and the tiger tamer stops in the middle when only two tigers had come across to the big stools to sit, and he gets the tigers back into their small cages on wheels very fast and takes them out toward the end of the tent, and we look at where people are pointing and screaming, and we see that the side of the tent is on fire.

The horses in the end rings see it, too, and the woman fights to control them but they break loose. They run toward one end, then wheel back and gallop toward the other.

The fire runs up the side fast like a lighted trail of gunpowder and races across the top, and it sweeps down to the far end of the tent so fast that people who had started to go out that way turn and start running back toward the other end, and they knock each other down and crush each other and get mixed up with the horses they are so scared.

The top of the tent has burned into a widening roaring hole with a black, curling edge, and flaming globs are falling down like meteors, sticking to whatever they hit and burning there. Everyone is screaming, and loud over the people screams is the shrieking neighing of the horses dashing wildly back and forth without caring about people being in the way, trampling them sometimes and then wheeling and galloping back or straight across the ring to the other side, making the people break and scream even more.

All of us rush down the bleachers to get to the ground, but it is crammed and people are shoving each other and stepping on each other and always screaming. The screaming is terrible. There are so many that we cannot get down off the bleachers.

The ropes are burning now, and one breaks and makes sparks as it swings to the ground. The tall poles that hold the roof up have caught fire. When we climb down a few rows, Doc says, "Come on" and he shows Ma and me how to slip between the foot planks and drop down onto the ground under the bleachers. It is a long fall, just like jumping out of a tree, but he catches me and then helps Ma down, and we run to the edge of the tent and then crawl under fast and get outside.

The air is swirling in dark-smelling, bitter smoke like a turpentine fire, and there are people running everywhere, men hollering, everybody scared and confused. Doc makes us move way back from the tent, and we turn and see the high smoke now and the tent has a big hole burned in the top, and some pieces are flying up into the air, rising up in the hot current of smoke. Other pieces fall into the tent, like pieces of wood going over a waterfall. The fire sound is like a high wind, a rushing storm wind blowing through maple trees, but frightening and dangerous. The tent looks ready to cave in, and far off we can hear some sirens coming, mixing with the screams of people.

Doc points up to the high flames and says, "Look there. He seems startled and says something to himself that I can't hear, a name or something, and he looks at Ma in a strange way. He puts both hands on her shoulders and almost yells at her: "It wasn't a dream, Anna," he says, and he steps back, his arms bent and his hands open toward her. "Maybe it wasn't a dream. Maybe the fire was real. I saw you save the roan!" He looks almost stunned. Ma seems bewildered. Her mouth is open but she doesn't speak.

"Ma?" I ask. "What's he mean?" She doesn't answer. "What's he doing?" Maybe with all the noise she doesn't hear me.

"You stay here!" he yells to us both, his hands held up in a stopping motion as he takes some steps backward toward the burning tent, but we can hardly hear him. Ma calls to him and then yells, "No!" but he turns and runs back to the edge where we had escaped and lifts it up as high as he can, almost to his waist, and even though he is coughing from the smoke and has his back to the opening and can hardly see, he calls and waves people to come out that way. A few run out bent over, but then nobody. Suddenly he bends down and looks under the flap, takes his shirt off, warps it around his head, and ducks back under.

The flap of the tent drops down again and we don't see him any more. Ma's face looks very worried, and she says he must have seen somebody who needed help. I think it was the horses.

Now the flames have run across the whole top and are steadily eating down toward unburned sides. People still run out one end of the tent like wild stampeding animals, and they stumble over the ones who fall and run right over them. Now and then a horse runs out, too, and everyone fights to get out of the way. Ma screams, "Doc!" and has fear in her eyes as she looks and looks to see where he comes out.

There is a big whooshing sound like a high wind-shift, and the whole top drops into the center, like the bank of a stream suddenly caving in when water wears it away, and the sides burst out with flames and smoke and a new worse screaming and crying comes from the people outside who scramble back away from the flames. The people who are under it cannot get out now someone shouts, and we still have not seen Doc. Everywhere the tent is on fire all the way to the ground, and the smoke is like burning pine trees.

It all seems to take about five minutes. I guess it was much longer than that, but it did not seem that way.

A person with an arm badge forces us go to a first aid station because we have soot on our faces and clothes, but they see that we are okay and Ma screams at them to let us go. Ma and me run back across the trampled grass and keep hunting around the edges of the fire as close as the firemen will let us, but we get stopped by fire trucks and hoses across the ground like fat gray snakes, and we circle back around the other way, Ma running now and calling all the time, her voice high and full of tears.

Suddenly a side of the tent gashes open and horses with green and yellow ribbons burst through, racing wildly right past the surprised firemen and out into the field, not stopping at all even when they are safe. Some circus hands run after them hollering and then not hollering, just running to stay close. I watch them go until they are very far away near a line of trees.

Fire pours through the break in the tent that the horses made, and the whole thing is gone now.

Ma searches with me until it is night, asking everybody we see, and a policeman comes up and asks us if we need help. Ma can hardly speak. He guesses that we lost somebody in the fire, and he takes us to a building near by where all the people who have lost someone are, and a woman takes down our information of who we are and who is missing. Then the circus people take us to a building near by where there are cots for the night and a person who comes in with news every now and then, but we don't sleep, and when it is still dawn-dark we go back out but there's nothing there, just the ring of stakes and workmen pulling the wrecked and smoldering pieces apart. The tent is gone, just smoking and blackened lumps and the three empty rings.

A workman covered in sooty black is talking in a loud voice to anyone who will listen. He seems very important. He tells us that the people who were inside are not able to be recognized. He says there must be close to two hundred who did not get out. He says that's a lucky figure. It could have been a lot worse.

Not for me.

A woman, the one from the tent last night, comes to us and asks if we are looking for a person named Anderson. "Yes," we both say, excited. She says there's a man who was rescued named Anderson and we should follow her. We do, walking fast through a jumble of hoses and ropes and tent pieces to get to the area they have for a first-aid station, getting more nervous and eager as we get nearer.

"Doc?" Ma calls, excited. "Doc?"

"There Mr. Anderson is," says the woman, "just in that third cot over there," and she points to a place where a big, heavy man lies with his arms burned and his eyes shut. "There's Daniel Anderson," says the woman, expecting us to be very happy.

"No," cries Ma. "No, no, no, no."

She sits down on a crate and cries and cries, and I hurt so much I can't even make tears come. It's just an ache in my chest, and I stand beside her and keep looking. I keep hoping. I run up and down the rows thinking I will find him in some other cot. It's no use. Finally she knows that. She knows there's nothing we can do.

The woman asks if we want to make a telephone call, and Ma says no, and the woman offers us some coffee and tells us how very sorry she is. We walk back across the field to the parking lot to our car, and when I turn to get in, it seems wrong just to leave. The smoke still trails into the sky in a few thin wisps, but now the whole field is flat where there used to be the big tent. I don't want to go, but Ma says we have to. There's no point in staying any longer.

We drive back home that afternoon, very slowly. I know it is hard for Ma to drive because she is crying to herself most of the way. She looks at me and shakes her head once, then pulls over to the side and cries for a long time. When we drive into the yard, Mrs. Strong comes rushing out. She has heard about the fire on the radio and says she has been frantic worrying about us, and I guess she was very scared when she did not know. She is so happy to see the car come in, and says she has news, that a woman named Devaney called and said she had found something about a boy who might be the one Doc is interested in. She says the person was very excited, and then Mrs. Strong looks into the car for the first time really and sees that Doc isn't there. And she knows.

She and Ma go out into the kitchen for a long time.

I go up to Doc's room and just sit there with his belongings. On his dresser are some of the things from our trip. I don't want to look at them at first, but then I want to touch them. There is the map that Mrs. Lake drew for us, a few old letters tied up in a bundle with string, his jack knife, a letter he was writing to Jeremy Danielson for his equipment to be shipped east, and notes he had written to himself when we were in the library in Strongsville.

On the last page of the lined yellow note pad there is just one thing written. It is a name. Augustus Jared Strong. Beside it is a big question mark written over and over in pencil. I close the pad and leave it on the dresser.

It is light when I wake up. Ma is touching me and tells me it is almost noon and time to get up. I'd been asleep on Doc's bed.

Closing

Cully

It is two weeks after the circus fire, and we have decided to put up a stone for Doc in the Strongs' little family cemetery. Mrs. Strong and Ma say it's all right because he was one of the family already. A man brings the stone to the house and he has carved on it just what Ma asked him to. It says: Gunnar "Doc" Anderson A Caring Man.

We put it in the ground one late afternoon. I don't have any words for all the tears we cried in the shadow of the great catalpa tree.

When we place the stone in the ground so that it stands up, I get a shoe box and dig a hole big enough for it, and in the shoe box I put the jack knife that Doc gave me and the hawk's feather. I wish I had more. He was the man I loved most and these were some things that meant a lot to him. The stone is right at the head of the box. I learned that you can dig a grave even if your eyes are filled by tears. You don't need to see the earth to know where it is.

This isn't like Pa's dying or any of the deaths in Weed. Doc isn't here. He just disappeared. But it still seems wrong, though, with no one to say any words for him. He would've liked to be on this land forever.

Ma chose the place for the stone, and she puts it beside the one for Augustus Jared Strong, a little boy, she says, who was one of her brothers who got lost. There is no minister and no speech. I can't say all I should, and finally I just look at Ma and say, "He was good to me" and Ma squeezes my shoulder. We just stand a while without saying anything more and hold each other as the sun goes down. The wind nearly stops and the tree's darkness covers us all.

EPILOGUE

A. J. Strong, II

That was the end of their journals. It was a puzzle, still. Two graves side by side but nobody in either one. Just names on headstones.

I searched the same records that Doc and Anna had scoured, read the books about the orphan trains and the New England Children's Aid Society, and I did all I could to fill in the gaps and solve the riddle of our family.

I found only one other small piece, a news item from the Chronicle which appeared in the summer about twelve years after Augustus disappeared. I include it here, with permission, in its entirety.

Farmer Reveals Secret

Coventry—Farmer Windham Rickenhauser confessed to this reporter yesterday that for more than ten years he has kept a secret. It's a small body he found and buried without telling anybody.

Rickenhauser's farm is in a remote section of Coventry, far down a dirt road off the main one that leaves Route 32 and heads toward the lake. "My ol' dog found him one day at the base of the stone wall, curled up and looking asleep. He was about seven—eight years old I'd guess. Still had on a work shirt and overalls and brown shoes. Stiffer'n a rail fence. Must've been dead more'n a week"

Rickenhauser said he asked around and then dug a grave right there and placed the boy's remains in it, covered it over, and used one of the stones from the wall to mark the place.

But now when he tried to find it for me, the wall had tumbled and the grave was lost. He could not describe the boy any further as his memory had grown hazy over the years.

The old farmer said he never heard of any missing child and he guessed the boy had simply gotten lost on a walk and starved to death within a half-mile of his farmhouse.

Why did he tell the story now? "'Cause I am getting near to passin' myself, and I don't want nobody wondering about that small pair of brown shoes on my mantel." He elaborated no further.

A search of Coventry records and interviews with Rickenhauser's neighbors failed to offer any further details to his story. The neighbors say he was somewhat eccentric and never wanted to have anything to do with the government, which may be why he never reported his discovery.

When I returned last week to ask Rickenhauser some follow-up questions, I found the house empty. The scuffed pair of boy's brown shoes was on the mantel, and beside them was a battered pair of worn work shoes. Apparently the old farmer, too, had "gone for a walk."

Some mysteries are not meant to be solved.

Augustus Jared Strong, II

"Stories are for joining the past to the future. Stories are for those late hours at night when you can't remember how you got from where you were to where you are. Stories are for eternity, when memory is erased, when there is nothing to remember except the story."

Tim O'Brien
The Things They Carried

Author's Note

Some of the characters in this story are based on people I knew or knew about, but they are blended here into composites and are not intended to portray any individual specifically. Any such results are coincidental only.

E.E.Sundt